ASH IS BACK…
and on her best behavior!

A night at the art gallery…
The clinking of wine glasses…
The hopeful thrill of a first date…
But <u>someone</u> has murder on their mind!

THE INCOMPLETE ARTIST

A life ended…
A fantasy cut short…

Detective Ashley Westgard
must set her disappointment aside,
flash her badge, and take command…
Because a killer is on the loose!

"THIS IS <u>MY</u> GALLERY NOW!"

ALSO BY PHILIP WYETH

Reparations USA
Reparations Mind
Reparations Core
Reparations Maze
Chasing the Best Days
Hot Ash and the Oasis Defect

The Incomplete Artist

PHILIP WYETH

Cover design by Philip Wyeth.

Official website:
www.philipwyeth.com

Ashley Westgard series website:
www.oasisdefect.com

CONTENTS

AUTHOR'S NOTE

I am a great admirer of the British spy master Len Deighton and his three *Bernard Samson* trilogies. What I as an author found of particular interest, and concern, was when he said, "The stories can be read in any order, and each one is complete in itself."

I have embraced the challenge implied in that statement while crafting this novel, which is only the second installment of what I hope will be a lengthy *Ashley Westgard* series. The task was daunting, considering the complexities that writing murder mysteries set within an imagined science-fiction future entail, as opposed to the very real Cold War which served as Mr. Deighton's backdrop.

Exploring the wide-ranging potentialities of life in 2045 will inevitably lead to world-building in each story, and here I made the conscious decision to not only dramatize new themes, but also express a distinctly different sensibility. Therefore, one might even describe *The Incomplete Artist* as being more Agatha Christie than Philip K. Dick, especially during the first half of the book.

I understand that some readers who now encounter the series for the first time, perhaps due to their affinity for female sleuths or the visual arts, might not be as interested in reading the more hard-boiled first book to familiarize themselves with Ash and her universe.

Which brings us back to Len Deighton. If he felt at liberty to share various illuminating tidbits at the start of *Spy Sinker* and *Faith*, then it might also prove beneficial for me to include some background information on the ambitious *Ashley Westgard* series.

The main conceit revolves around several major technological breakthroughs which take place in 2025, and are collectively referred to as the Trifecta. Automation and drug decriminalization combine to jump-start a green industrial revolution by utilizing hemp-powered, self-replicating machines called Worker-Factory-Mechanics.

At the same time, artificial wombs and the pinnacle of women's empowerment shift society toward matriarchal rule. A rotating body of international female leaders known as the Essential Planners oversees a sweeping worldwide build-out and cleanup project as facilitated by the WFMs.

When series opener *Hot Ash and the Oasis Defect* begins, humanity has been on this idealistic path for twenty years. But now the first cracks are starting to show, just as a younger and more spoiled generation inherits the reins from the original visionaries.

A new malaise has taken root…

Our eyes and ears during this perilous moment in time belong to Detective Ashley Westgard of the Jacksonville Police Corps. A knockout blond with grave work responsibilities but also terrible personal vices, she is both a beneficiary and victim of this decadent age. As she pursues the killers who defy *and* belie the would-be Utopia of 2045, Ash must overcome her own flaws and weaknesses in order to solve each case.

This future world is bursting with exciting creative possibilities, and I plan to explore the many philosophical and existential implications while always staying grounded in the tactile urgency of a criminal investigation.

So as you now turn the page and begin reading *The Incomplete Artist*, consider the following questions: What do *you* think the function and purpose of the visual arts will be in a time when robots can be programmed to mimic the great masters? And who will have the courage to declare themselves creatively relevant when surrounded by an army of titanium Picassos?

-Philip Wyeth
Los Angeles, CA
March 2021

1. THE CONNOISSEUR

"I welcome you to the ball!"

Thomas Templeton smiled and cast his right arm forward as the glass double doors slid open. Detective Ash Westgard of the Jacksonville Police Corps, off-duty and dressed to kill, took his other arm and together they entered Muir Gallery.

As a second set of doors yielded, they came upon a lively scene of patrons dressed in fancy attire strolling among the many works of art on display. A string quartet recording could be heard through the festive din of glasses clinking, friends reacquainting, and growing excitement over these fine examples of craftsmanship which would soon be sold at auction.

"This is overwhelming," Ash said. "Where do we even start?"

"I don't know if you prefer sculptures or paintings," Thomas replied, "but I'm inclined to look in on the bar first."

"I agree."

After they were served, Thomas raised his slender flute of champagne and said, "Cheers to you, m'lady."

"Game on."

"Now please, Ashley, follow my lead."

He took her by the hand and began to navigate across the bustling showroom.

"Thomas?! Is that you?" a voice called from within the throng.

A man in his late fifties with wispy white hair and circular blue spectacles fought his way toward them.

"Braxton, my goodness! There you are indeed," Thomas said as the two grabbed each other's biceps affectionately.

"How are you, old chap? I had no idea you were on the mainland."

"I wouldn't miss this night of pitiless bidding wars for the world. Besides, it will most certainly stave off the boredom."

"*And* get the heart rate going," Braxton said as he examined Ash's low-cut silver dress from over the frames of his glasses.

"For those of us who still have them," Thomas said slyly. "Braxton, allow me to introduce Miss Ashley Westgard. She was in fact the only interesting person I met at that ghastly to-do some local law enforcement charity held last week."

The other man took Ash's hand into his own and gently rubbed the top with his thumb as he spoke.

"Well, Miss Westgard, it's a pleasure to meet you. Braxton O'Shea, at your service. Lover of all sunrises and sunsets, particularly when seated in quiet comfort along an ocean shore. But of course, sometimes imagined coastlines must also suffice."

He tilted his head in the direction of a large, three-dimensional tropical scene on display nearby.

Ash freed her hand from O'Shea's grip and smiled politely. She said, "Nice to meet you as well. So, how do you and Thomas know each other?"

Both men chuckled, and Braxton tapped a fingertip against his chin while adding, "Us island boys are a rare breed. We always find our own kind."

Ash raised her eyebrows at Thomas, whose wavy light-brown bangs jostled as he shook his head. "What an exaggerator you are, Mister Brax! No, no, Ashley, there's nothing scandalous or otherwise suspicious hidden within his cryptic words. What he really means, is that we are the last of the vanguard of *old* money."

"The Loafers of the Caribbean," Braxton said with a grin as he sipped at his drink.

"Golf... tennis... croquet. All the leisurely trappings of pre-twenty-first-century life." Thomas swept his arm around the gallery. "Which is why we anachronisms find ourselves right at home here tonight."

"And I dare say, you've found *her*," Braxton quipped. "Now, Ashley—"

"Ash," she said firmly.

"By all means. Tell me, *Ash*, what were you doing at that boring and boorish affair to which Thomas just alluded?"

"I'm a cop, actually. I was invited."

Braxton's arm gave an involuntary start, which caused the ice cubes inside his tumbler to clink loudly.

Ash said, "Are you surprised, Mr. O'Shea? Not all of us on the force have beer bellies—or internal wiring."

Thomas added, "Ash is being incredibly modest right now. She is in fact a homicide detective second-grade with the JPC. So I hope for your sake that you've established alibis for the many skeletons in your closet."

Braxton O'Shea brought a hand to his breast and patted the lapel of his suit jacket, offering a bow as he said, "Detective, no offense intended. I simply had no idea that anyone involved in the *serious* professions, those that help keep our world afloat, would ever cross paths with such a lazybones as Mr. Templeton here. Not to mention spending time in his company voluntarily, hahaha."

The man let out a hearty stuttering laugh as he slapped Thomas on the shoulder.

"If we're being brutally honest," Ash said, "Thomas was only the *second*-most interesting part of the gala."

"You see," Thomas said, "we happened to meet at the punch bowl about halfway through all those ponderous speeches. Priorities, priorities!" He flicked a finger against his friend's nearly empty glass.

"Speaking of which," Ash and Braxton said virtually in unison, and all three began to laugh.

"Shall we?" Thomas said.

Together the group made its way back toward the bar.

A short while later, after Braxton wandered off and they mingled briefly with several other patrons, Ash found herself alone with Thomas in a corner of the room.

He did look dapper in his "anachronistic" outfit of navy blazer, gingham shirt with no tie, tan slacks, and leather deck shoes. It was a style of dress that had matured over the course of a century: that thrown-together look which was undergirded by a vast fortune, as worn by the playboy, the dandy, the man without a care in the world—but whose education and pedigree made underestimating him a dangerous proposition. As for resisting him…

It truly was an opposites-attract moment when they met one week ago. Ash had been driven to liquor-thirst by the tedious philanthropic event whose invitation she was *supposed* to see as a high honor: the chance to hobnob alongside JPC top brass, in lieu of the public commendation they couldn't give her for cracking a murder case with far-reaching implications two months ago.

So she had quietly bowed out from the round table that she shared with, among other notables, her immediate superior, the Chief of Detectives Gabriela Paraquez. Then she killed some time in the ladies room, first applying fresh eyeliner before adjusting her mauve long dress. *That* exquisite outfit had been anything but thrown together, and Ash looked like a movie star on awards night when she reemerged and stopped under the lobby's twinkling chandeliers to order herself a vodka-tonic.

But the thirty-something man she saw standing alone at the bar, and who was very carefully twisting a sliver of orange peel above a glass, seemed not in the least affected by her dramatic entrance.

"Excuse me," he said finally, after breaking his concentration and submerging the peel. "Would you be so kind as to taste this? I'm trying to teach that infernal barkeep how to make a proper old-fashioned. Sadly, my instructions seem to be falling on deaf ears."

Ash took a step closer, eyeing the tuxedo-clad robot that stood behind the counter as she received the glass. She took a small sip.

"Hmm. You're right. It's not quite there."

"Damn," the man muttered. "You'd think at a ritzy affair like this, they would account for all the popular recipes *plus* a few variations. But who do I blame, the bureaucrats or the machines?"

Ash hailed the bot-tender, which rolled toward her silently.

"Yes, ma'am," it said in a gracious, watery voice. "May I take your order?"

She glanced sidelong at her new acquaintance and said, "The secret, I find, is to get something that's foolproof. Shot of tequila," she told the robot. A smile curved up the corner of her mouth. "Make that two."

"As you wish." The bot produced two tiny glasses and began to pour from a nozzle in its left forearm.

She heard the man chuckle. He said, "Do you really expect me to tarnish my palate with worm killer, right after I've humiliated this talking fountain by forcing it to make me three drinks in a row?"

Ash held both shot glasses aloft. She smirked. "Don't think I can't—or won't—take care of these all by myself."

"I never doubted your abilities. Besides, how could I? I know nothing about you."

She downed one of the tequilas, then made as if to offer him the other, before drinking that as well.

"You do now," she said in a deadpan voice, feeling utterly self-satisfied as the dueling shots snaked through her with a fiery sizzle.

The man quietly set his old-fashioned down, ordered a tequila for himself, drank it without fanfare, and then turned away from her in the direction of the main hall. Without thinking, Ash ran after him and grabbed his sleeve.

He looked at her curiously and said, "*Excuse

me," then dusted off his blazer and continued walking.

While Ash—shocked, furious, *rejected*—was summoning all of her willpower not to assault a stranger at such a prestigious event, she saw the man pause mid-stride and pivot back towards her.

"I do believe you'll be needing this," he said, reaching into his jacket pocket and handing her a business card.

She glanced at it and read, "Thomas MacLeish Templeton. Connoisseur of all things fine," then called out after him, "Ash… My name's Ash."

"Very good," she heard him say as he receded with a wave, knowing instantly that her own words had sounded more like a plea than a declaration.

The connoisseur had won the first round. And it had taken Ash nearly a week to corral him into spending an evening together at the gallery—his idea, of course—where they would attend a live auction featuring works by some of the best talents within Jacksonville's flourishing art scene.

But Detective Ashley Westgard knew what it took to break a case—and a man. Somehow, she'd make this suave Thomas Templeton reveal what he was truly made of beneath his own *fine* airs…

2. MOVEMENT 24

As they finished their first circuit around the gallery, having given the pieces on display only a cursory glance while spending most of that time socializing, Ash was now getting a better sense of the building's layout.

The rectangular main showroom was wide open like a convention center hall, and therefore could be configured in any number of ways depending on the desired effect. Tonight, in addition to the free-flowing pathways between the various works and exhibits, space had also been allocated for coat-check, a bar, and a catering station.

At each end of the long wall facing the gallery's front entrance was a large swinging door that remained closed. And in between, a normal set of double doors opened onto a carpeted room which was filled with rows of padded chairs. Silver stanchions and crimson velvet ropes barred the threshold.

"When the clock strikes seven and the auctions

begin," Thomas informed her, "that is where hearts will soar or be crushed depending on who wins."

Ash said, "Does that include yourself? I'd hate to see you cry on our first date."

"Ha! I'm prepared for any outcome—win, lose, or *draw* a tissue to wipe my eyes."

"So you're the sensitive type, eh?"

"Just being realistic. Professional golfers often grind for years without winning a single tournament. I'll survive if I end up going home empty-handed tonight."

"Even without *me?*"

Ash smiled mischievously and took a backwards step away from Thomas, but in the process ended up colliding with someone who was walking past at that moment.

"What on earth!" a large woman wrapped in a fringed shawl cried out. But then, after regaining her composure, she said, "I don't believe my eyes… If it isn't Thomas Templeton himself gracing us with his presence once again."

"Hello, Carmella," Thomas bellowed as he leaned in to kiss the woman's cheek. "I've been looking forward to this for weeks."

"How wonderful to hear! And besides, I can't very well support the entirety of M-24 all by myself. Especially not now, when the school has gained four new recruits since our last big event six months ago."

"Is that right? My congratulations! But first things first, you must welcome into the fold an auction novice. Ash Westgard, please say hello to Carmella Edelweiss, the benefactress most responsible for all that you see here tonight."

"Sorry for bumping into you like that," Ash said. She offered her hand and felt the matron's fingers clamp down onto her own like the jaws of a terrier.

"Oh, it's no bother," Edelweiss said. "Better me than one of the sculptures, because at least *I* won't shatter if I go tumbling down onto the floor, haha!"

"I guess that's true. But still, I'll be more careful."

"So tell me, is Thomas being a proper tour guide?"

"We only just arrived. I'm trying to take it all in."

"Well, I do hope you'll also *take* something home with you later tonight. We must all do our part to keep the *hors d'oeuvres* flowing."

Edelweiss laughed as she plucked a spinach-and-cheese cracker from the tray being held aloft by a passing tuxedo-clad caterer.

"Tut-tut," Thomas said as Carmella munched happily. "We mustn't take advantage of the uninitiated. No, these proceedings are only for the sake of Ashley's entertainment and education."

"Pardon my impertinence, you're absolutely right." Edelweiss dabbed at her lips with a napkin, then turned to Ash and said, "I sometimes forget that not *everyone* knows about, let alone swears allegiance to the M-24 credo. Has Mr. Templeton at least enlightened you, or did the rogue drag you in here without a proverbial paddle?"

"He did mention a few things about the group," Ash said. "Let's see… No working with robots, and something about leaving part of the paper blank?"

"Precisely! We are a humans-first guild rooted in the tools and methods that pre-date our reliance on high technology. Particularly prior to the Trifecta, whose consequences have led the arts far astray these last twenty years. And as for the other aspect you mentioned, that in actuality is our signature move, and so important in the symbolic sense because what it represents far exceeds the act itself. Can you guess why?"

Ash shook her head.

"Consider," the woman said patiently, "how the deliberately unfinished work can *only* be accomplished by a human being. No painting machine would ever *think* to stop before the programmed task was complete. So whenever you catch sight of an empty space or truncated appendage tonight, understand that this detail is a flag raised boldly in defense of the species itself."

"I'll keep on the lookout," Ash said.

"Good, because Movement 24 is putting the whole world on notice. We're not afraid to take risks and stand on our own two feet—or hands, as it were—while striving for greatness in this age of atrophy. I declare, despite the encroaching monster that is automation, resilience and gusto will never lose their currency!"

"Come now, Carmella," Thomas said with mild reproach. "Don't scare the poor girl off. Why, you're nearly frothing at the mouth! Did success go to your head, or have you become a fanatic since I last saw you?"

"Well, you did say this was her first time here! Why wouldn't I *download* M-24's prospectus into her brain?" Edelweiss finally took a calming breath, then said, "Everything I do comes from a place of *love*. Remember, it was *people* who survived famine and disease and war, and then established the stable conditions necessary to even make the AI revolution possible. We did the work, so why should we slink off the stage now and let a bunch of soulless *gadgets* get all the glory?"

"I know, but tonight we're supposed to be celebrating that triumph, right?"

"Yes, certainly. However, since I have your lady friend's ear, I must be certain that she understands exactly *where* she is! It is a hollow inheritance for a civilization to self-euthanize after its most brilliant flash, and I for one cannot abide sitting on the mausoleum shelf, not while *I* still feel so thrillingly alive!"

Thomas gently lowered Carmella's shaking fist as he said, "Okay, I can see that we've gotten you terribly excited. It's much too early for that kind of fire and brimstone, especially considering that you haven't even sold anything yet! Let us not ascend the mountain before our creations have borne any fruit."

"Yes, you're correct. I will try to calm down. But we're due for something momentous tonight, I can just feel it, darling!"

"Ashley and I will applaud you later, when you take a victory lap."

Edelweiss blew a double kiss and waltzed over to the nearest appetizer tray.

"She was feisty," Ash said once the other woman was out of earshot.

"Carmella has a tremendous passion for the arts," Thomas replied while gazing around the gallery. "It knows no bounds. Don't be surprised if you see more of that *joie de vivre* on display from the others as well."

"Fine with me. It's kind of adorable, actually. And you say she set this whole place up?"

"Not solely by herself, but as a driving force her bucks *and* her brawn were offered in equal measure. Now, speaking of displays," Thomas said while trying to suppress a grin, "what do you think of this one?"

Ash beheld a giant replica walnut shell. Mounted on a one-foot metal base, it rose up to the top of her head and was cracked open wide down the center seam. Dozens of slits allowed in additional light, and inside she could see a number of tropical birds perched on tree branches.

"Uh… I guess it seems well done. But the shell, that can't be real wood, right?"

"No, no," Thomas said. "Some sort of plaster or composite material that was chiseled and painted for realistic effect. What does it say to you?"

Ash glanced at the information placard. It read: *Loyalty's Treasures* by Samantha L. Minn.

"I mean, it *looks* nice, but still… Why?"

Thomas could no longer contain his pleasure at Ash's bewilderment and let out a laugh. He patted her on the back affectionately and said, "I've known Sammy for quite a while, so let me offer you a few insights into her creative journey."

"Please do."

"The first step any artist takes on a new road is as innocent as it is blind. Along the way, she may encounter sights both good and bad—majestic peaks as well as dark paths that tempt her curious and eager mind with offers of esoteric knowledge. But—" Thomas raised an emphatic finger. "Sometimes… Well, too often really… Sometimes an artist will get hung up on a detail which works best only when functioning as part of the greater whole. Obsession can set in, and then this promising artist will inexplicably fixate upon that minor element as if it were the central theme itself."

Ash indicated the beige monstrosity that loomed large before them. "I take it your friend has more pieces like this?"

"And how! A few years ago, Samantha was merrily reconstructing some famous still-life paintings in order to improve her eye and technique. Within six months, however, her studio looked like a giant bowl of mixed nuts."

"Did you or anyone else try to do an

intervention? Or is that not how this art stuff works?"

"Why should we?" Thomas laughed. "Ms. Minn is doing quite well for herself, as you will see shortly once the auctions begin. This period of her career might not be *my* cup of tea, but one has to admire the commitment."

"And the birds?" Ash coaxed.

"Maybe you should ask Samantha."

"She's *here?* The artist herself?"

"Of course! Soaking up the praise—and perplexed looks—is half the fun for these lofty minds so burdened with transmuting the eternal mysteries into something both tangible... and purchasable. Tonight is their well-deserved break from that routine of meditative isolation."

"Will she be insulted if I don't understand?"

"Not at all! Besides, these quirky and unexpected detours usually start in good faith, with no malice or dysfunction implied. Do you think that's not possible, or funny? Listen, I know a writer who once nearly had a nervous breakdown over the use of hyphens. 'I'm putting them everywhere!' he cried while holding up several pages of a manuscript."

"And?"

"It was indeed a dreadful sight! Gave old Céline and his million ellipses a run for their money. But the point of this," Thomas said deliberately, "is to explain how *the characteristics of the craft* can usurp *the purpose of the task*. By strictly adhering to the rules and traditions, or thinking only about style and method... You can easily lose your way, even when motivated by the best of intentions."

"So what happened to this writer friend of yours?" Ash said.

"He finally did what every creative person ought

to do, and got a second opinion! Which for him meant trusting in a good editor's discretion, and the rest is history. For my friend, who shall remain unnamed, is readable once again. But let us fly away from this perch. There's a piece over in the far corner I've been dying to see in person."

"Do you think you might bid on it?" Ash asked a few minutes later, after they had stopped in front of a painting which several others were also admiring. The canvas was a four-foot-high perfect triangle, and the desert horizon design drew the eye toward a red gemstone at its center point.

Thomas puckered his mouth. "Mum's the word. I *never* reveal my objectives in advance."

"Come on. I wanna know what you like." Ash sidled up against his body.

"Nice try, you little flirt. But silence saves money. Funds which later on might even serve to benefit you, in fact."

Ash grinned. "I like the sound of that! So have it your way, Mr. Poker Face. Now let's go look at a few things that caught *my* eye."

"Oh yes, let's. I always find it refreshing to learn what the layman considers quality art."

"You're not calling me average, are you, Tommy?" Ash ran her tongue over her teeth. "A commoner?"

"Hardly! My dear, if you knew how flabbergasted I often find myself at the vapid state of this world, you would understand just how starved I am for anything *uncommon*."

Ash couldn't tell whether Thomas was being playful, sincere, or condescending—and by the time she realized that her temper was flaring up, it was already too late…

"Ah, gimme a break," she said grumpily. "I don't care if you're rich. Doesn't mean I have to act like it's a big honor just to be in your royal presence."

Thomas was momentarily taken aback, but then placed two gentle fingers inside the crook of her elbow. He said calmly, "On the contrary, Miss Westgard. It is *my* honor to have met you. Now please, lead the way…"

Ash moved slowly forward, feeling herself float as her head cooled and began to tingle with delight. This Thomas Templeton was something new. An unknown quantity. He didn't try to match her blow for blow, but parried her every challenge with stoic grace.

As she led him by the hand across the room, she secretly hoped that he also knew the right time and place to lose all control.

3. ADIEU

"And what do we have here?"

Thomas indicated a life-size portrait which nearly a dozen people had gathered around and were discussing loudly. Ash squeezed in to get a closer look.

The painting featured a slender female cyberpunk with spiky short brown hair wearing a sleeveless black skinsuit. Her right hand was raised in an open-palmed military salute, while her left was robotic and gripped a narrow paintbrush like a pencil.

"Who's the girl?" Ash asked.

"None other than the creator of this bold piece. Which is called…" Thomas leaned in toward the wall and squinted. "*Adieu*. Hmm."

"And her name?"

"Marta Gionet. She's around here somewhere, I'm sure."

"Why's it getting people so riled up? Look at them, they're going wild."

"That's a good question," Thomas said. "Uh… Oh, here's someone who ought to know."

Just then a ruggedly handsome man with close-cropped sandy blond hair pushed his way through the group and faced the painting. He scowled and mashed his fists into the pockets of his brown tweed sport coat while turning away.

"Stan!" Thomas called out to him. "How are you, good sir?"

"Not expecting to get into a civil war," the man growled as he approached. Then, noticing Ash for the first time, he mustered a smile and said, "Thomas, how have you been?"

"Well, very well. Stanley Bennett, please make the acquaintance of Ash Westgard."

"How's it going, Ash?"

"I'm fine, thanks." She looked over at the painting. "Not your favorite?"

Bennett shook his head. "Ah… no. Thomas, do you see why I'd like to take a blowtorch to it?"

Templeton fiddled with one of his shirt buttons for a moment, then said, "It doesn't seem that out of the ordinary to me. Marta's always been fascinated with herself."

"Ha!" A woman who very much resembled the subject of the painting came near. In a throaty French accent she added, "It's because I am saying *adieu* in real life that Stanley doesn't like it."

The woman simulated slicing off her left arm and pretended to toss it aside.

"Now Marta," Thomas said, "surely you're not considering heavy bodily modification? You've trained that hand since you were a child."

Stanley Bennett spoke up. He said, "No, it's worse than that. Apparently she's decided to leave M-24 to go off on her own—and chose *tonight* as her coming out party."

"That's correct," Marta said proudly. "This will be the last painting to come from my flesh alone. I am ready for another challenge… as I work *with* the machines."

Thomas said, "But Marta darling, that's heresy!" He looked back and forth between the two artists. "I am simply shocked, as I'm sure everyone else is. How on earth did this all come about?"

Marta ran her fingers back through her hair, then said, "I don't mean to upset anyone, but it represents more than me leaving our school. I want to *lead* the next phase of artistry by influencing the robots myself. Otherwise, if we leave it to the scientists, they'll never get it right. Humanity and aesthetics would both suffer in consequence."

Stanley's face was red. He said, "You could've just walked away then. But to go out like this on everyone else's night… Wait, let me guess, you're hoping others will follow? Which really makes this stunt a recruitment exercise."

Marta flashed a smile. "Maybe. Why does it matter so much? *You* didn't start M-24. You only joined us as part of your own journey. I think you're just jealous because I'm the one who's leaving first."

Ash had so many questions but she didn't want to intrude on the conversation. Instead she glanced up at Thomas, and he took the hint.

"Please, you two, can we not kiss and make up? We all know that Marta has a flair for the dramatic. I wouldn't expect anything less, if tonight is indeed her swan song."

"Oh, Thomas," Marta said. "You've always been so understanding of your artist friends."

Bennett was still fuming, however. He said, "Fine, be a bitch and try to steal the show. I can see your true colors clearly. It's Marta the opportunist, now off to chase a new trend by grooming titanium

Picassos!"

Marta reached for his hand but he pulled it away. She said with genuine emotion, "Stanley, you must believe me! We all go through different seasons in our lives. I truly feel the universe is telling me to embrace this great responsibility, of trying to weave together cold technology with the beating heart of creation. Will you not give me your blessing? I admire you and your work so dearly."

Bennett looked at the painting again and said, "You can put a million credits in my pocket or fly me around the world for a commission, but there are some compromises I'll never make. The artificial, which came second, cannot be the *source* of anything. A robot will never get hit by a bolt of creative lightning—or realize afterward that the eureka moment had been a lie. These are crucial parts of the process that you can't fake! But you know, Marta, just go and do whatever it is you think you should. Hope you make some money tonight."

He walked off and disappeared into the crowd.

Thomas finally broke the silence. He said, "Miss Gionet, no matter what the truth may be, I wish you the best of luck in your future endeavors. You are one of a kind."

Marta gave a modest bow. "Thank you, *mon amour*. Change is always so difficult. And I apologize to the lady for having to witness such an unfortunate scene. This first impression must cast us both in a terrible light."

"Oh, I'm sure she's encountered much worse than your little spat with Stanley," Thomas said as he laughed mildly. "For you see, Lady Ash works for the police department."

"She has a *day job?* Really! But she's so gorgeous, I could paint her for months and never tire of it. Would you take me up on the offer to perhaps sit while I sketch you, Ash? I promise, it will be less dangerous than dragging criminals back to the jailhouse."

"That sounds fun," Ash said, "but I'm not sure I want to tempt fate by having you draw me with a mechanical arm. There's already enough bots working at JPC as it is. Plus… aren't you moving away from painting people?"

"Not necessarily. But *training* robots, yes. I'm trying to break through the rigid barriers, so they can understand concepts like discretion and the value of beautiful chance. I don't know that I will be successful, or how long it might take, but I am convinced that only someone from Movement 24 could hope to achieve it."

Ash nodded her head. "Okay, now I'm starting to see what this is all about. Thomas had mentioned to me on the ride over that your group's name somehow related to the Trifecta."

"Yes, because we feel a profound nostalgia for the year 2024. It was the last time people were fully in control of their own destiny."

"I get that part, but… Why are *you* doing this now?"

Marta set her jaw and declared, "I am but one woman. I don't have the power to stop something which began twenty years ago. So I pursue my deepest concern instead. Even if artist colonies like ours are never actually threatened, the world itself might forget that *people magic* is what makes so much possible. To me, that would signify the quiet death of our industrious nature. Then what will be left for the future artists working in '64 and '84? Perhaps M-24 is correct to build walls, but my heart tells me I must design a better style of bridge."

Thomas said, "Marta, if you're motivated by such a noble goal, then I must salute you for embarking upon the undertaking so gallantly. Bravo!"

"*Merci*, Thomas! I have to go now and talk to these other people who have been waiting so patiently, but perhaps I will see you both later on."

"There she goes," Thomas said to Ash as Marta approached the group that was discussing her painting in earnest. "The freest spirit of all."

"And a girl who knows what she wants."

"Your kindred soul?"

"Could be," Ash said as she tapped one of her earrings. "I *do* know I want another drink."

"How about that?" Thomas said. "You and I both seem to want all the same things. Oh, waiter!"

4. A NEW NEED

It seemed to Ash as if they couldn't go fifteen feet without running into someone that Thomas knew very well. Just now, he and another man his age were playfully hurling insults back and forth while concluding their brief reunion.

"You're a real popular guy," she said a moment later.

"These are my people," he replied. "And this is our night."

Thomas took in a big breath, closed his eyes, and then exhaled dramatically. He smiled.

"Yes. I am *home*."

Ash felt a wave of goodness wash over her. She was so used to being lied to while doing her job, that hearing a person speak genuinely sometimes caught her off guard.

She said, "Thanks for inviting me in."

"Feeling cozy so far?"

"Mm-hmm."

"Great, now—"

A woman in a purple sequin dress drew near and held up a bulky antique camera. She pointed it at them and said playfully, "Say Gouda!" The bulb flashed and then she quickly jumped in front of another group to repeat the process.

Thomas's eyes suddenly lit up. He said, "There's Samantha! I knew we'd find her eventually."

He raised his hand high and waved at a woman whose long skirt swayed as she crossed the room.

"Hello, Sammy!" he called.

She stopped abruptly and turned on the heel of her boot, then smiled when she saw Thomas and bounded over to give him a pinch on the cheek.

"Hey, Tom-Tom! Long time no see, huh?"

"I know, I know. You can't get enough of me." Thomas then said to Ash, "We met for coffee two days ago. Now Ash, please give Samantha your impressions of her *nutty* creation."

As Ash tapped her chin in thought, the other woman folded her arms and gave a curious smirk.

"Well… I'm no expert, but I might be willing to *shell* out a few credits for it."

Samantha clapped her hands giddily. "I always love meeting my fans," she said with a wink. "Any friend of Tom's is a friend of mine."

Ash leaned in to meet the hug that Samantha offered, and smelled a zesty lilac emanating from her body.

"Lovely perfume," she said. "What's the line?"

"DIY, maybe? I'm pulling your leg. I actually craft my own scents from natural oils." Samantha reached into her canvas tote bag and fished out a tiny spray bottle that had no label. "See?"

"Ah, very cool."

"Drop by my loft sometime. We girls can get to know each other and then whip up an aroma that suits you and you alone."

Ash said, "Thomas, your friends have so many talents!"

"What can I say," he guffawed, "I only surround myself with the best."

"I like her," Samantha said as she gave Ash's hand a light squeeze.

"As do I," Thomas mused.

"Now you two, I hate to run off, but there's so many people to visit with on these big nights."

"Of course. We'll try to enter your orbit again later, when you'll no doubt need help transporting your newfound riches home."

"Oh, stop! Look who's calling who moneybags. You're outrageous, Mr. Templeton, and that's why I adore you. Have fun, you cute little lovebirds."

"Ha!" Thomas hollered as Samantha skittered away. "I believe it is *you* who loves birds."

She flapped her arms like wings and then leaned onto the shoulders of two people who were part of a larger group.

Ash glanced down at her hand, then shaped it into a beak and cawed at Thomas, "Polly wanna vodka?"

He made chicken elbows and said, "Quickly, let us fly to the *nestillery*."

Ash rolled her eyes. "You… are ridiculous. I'm gonna order something nasty to make you gag on all those puns."

"Gag, gargle, and grin. Hmm. Perhaps instead of vodka, I'll order a gin!"

"Oh my god. You need to shut up."

Thomas shook a wing. "Make me?"

Ash lifted her purse momentarily, then let it drop against her body.

"Damn. I forgot my taser."

"While you scrounge up some other form of weapon, I might venture to the facilities for a brief respite. Then drinks?"

"Sure thing."

As Thomas worked his way through the crowd, Ash began to meander around looking at some of the pieces she hadn't noticed before. There was a sequence of tiny animal carvings encased in protective glass. A full set of candy-striped kitchenware, each with matching surface chips. A painting of a frail old woman playing the violin...

"If it isn't the preacher and the salesman," she heard a voice say sarcastically over her shoulder.

Curious, Ash pivoted around while feigning interest in another piece, and saw Stanley Bennett with beer in hand standing next to a man and a woman who were both in late middle age.

"We are here to glorify the likes of you," the woman said, nodding solemnly.

"Which one am I again?" the other man added with a laugh. He was wearing a shimmering black tuxedo and had gelled his sparse graying hair with great care.

"Oh Roger, you know how much poor Stanley suffers on nights like these. The sheer galling hypocrisy of having to transact transcendence. Heaven forbid the rest of us mere mortals enjoy ourselves while absorbing some of their radiance."

"Who said I'm enjoying myself?" Roger quipped. "I've got to stage-manage this whole operation. Maybe later, after all is said and done."

"See, Stanley?" the woman said. "You're not the only one who's feeling on edge, so please relax. Besides, I helped reel in some of this crowd, so why shouldn't I sip a little champagne?"

Bennett sighed. "I guess you're right, Daphne. And hey, what's the only thing better than having a critical eye? Receiving a critic's blessing!" He gulped some of his drink and added, "You got the flock to show up at church, now let's hope they do their part and load up the collection plate."

"Which reminds me," Daphne said, "I ought to have a few nibbles before the fun begins. Ta-ta!"

As the woman stepped away, Ash also kept herself moving while trying to remain within range of the conversation.

"Something else on your mind, Stan?" Roger asked.

"Always. But don't worry about it. The show must go on, right?"

"Most definitely. Including for me. Back to work, back to schmoozing…"

A moment later, Ash and Stanley Bennett were face to face.

"You again," he said. "Ash, was it?"

"Yep."

"Did you hear all that?"

"Maybe," she said with a smile. "Not having a great night?"

"That was just inside baseball. Roger does a good job running the gallery. And Daphne… Well, she's been in the business longer than I've been alive. Open houses and auctions are her whole world."

"But not you?"

"They're alright. Part of the deal, I guess."

"So what *do* you live for?"

Bennett said, "You really want to know? Or what?"

Ash could feel his eyes boring into her. It wasn't lust or even the artist sizing her up as a possible subject. This was a *force*—one that could be pointed in any direction, but never reduced in intensity.

"Tell me," she said.

"Okay then. There's what I want, what I need,

and what I need to do."

"How do you know which to go for first?"

"I wasn't completely joking when I called this place a church. God *is* here, or should be."

"And you artists play the part of God?"

"Some think they do. And plenty of other people hang around telling them it's true."

"But you disagree?"

Stanley straightened his posture. He said, "First you have to ask, what does art mean when a machine can paint your portrait in any famous style you want? I believe it can still benefit people's lives in ways that go far beyond assembly lines and barber schools. Which explains why, despite all the computing power at its disposal, the inorganic hive mind still hasn't come up with one new aesthetic technique. It can't do what I do: put something that has never existed before onto a blank piece of paper."

"That sounds pretty godlike to me," Ash said.

"People only think about Acts of God in terms of creation and destruction. I'm saying that God encompasses much, much more. God is *no*. God is *tomorrow*. God is patience and restraint. And not out of masochistic self-denial, either. It's so we can harness all the energy that's inside us with the impact of the bow and arrow. My job as an artist is to take proper aim."

"That's deep." Ash paused, then said, "Why are you so against Marta wanting to work with robots?"

Bennett said, "You know about M-24's calling card, right?"

"The unfinished work, you mean?"

"Exactly. It's not just a cheap way for us to get people's attention. The creative process is inherently subjective, because there are countless potential forks in the road while you work on each piece.

These are fateful decisions that every artist must make. But robots standing in front of an easel can only obey what's written in the code of their operating system. They never pause to think in the middle of a brushstroke. Only humans experience doubt. Only *we* have free will. M-24 highlights that essential distinction through the act of abstaining. Bottom line, I'd rather be incomplete than obsolete."

Ash said, "By that, do you mean it's your want or your need?"

He thought for a moment, then said, "Art is what I *have* to do. And the more I paint the better I get, so there's even less time to think about what I want. I'm the bow as well as the archer now."

"Maybe Marta feels the same way. By listening to what her heart says she's supposed to do."

"Her new need?" Bennett nodded slowly. "It's possible. I just hope she doesn't waste years of her life on a fool's errand, when her own style would keep developing otherwise. I want what's best for *her*, because it benefits us all."

"I guess only God knows the answer to that."

"Then let's pray Marta's aim is true."

Ash caught sight of Thomas's head bobbing among the crowd. Walking with him was an older man with broad shoulders and meticulously sculpted sideburns. They beckoned for her to approach.

"Thanks for the art lesson," she said to Stanley.

"Of course," he replied. "See you around."

5. THE DIVINE FEMININE

Thomas pointed out two paintings which were staged fifteen feet apart. One depicted a slice of rural life, while the other was an abstract rendering of brass musical instruments.

He said, "Two artists with vastly different takes on the world... or how they think it should be. Would you believe that they both started out under the tutelage of the same master during their apprenticeships?"

Ash spent a moment reading the information provided about each piece, then said, "But they're both part of M-24, it looks like. I can clearly see the blank spots. So... ?"

"Today they're in agreement philosophically, yes. But early on is usually when creatives begin to assert themselves stylistically. They might react viscerally to the professional whose works they've been tasked with facilitating—and in time, seek to define their own boldly unique vision."

Ash studied the brightly painted outdoor scene.

Five young women were standing in a field and singing with their arms spread wide, while livestock grazed under a clear sky. It was about as far from her own lived experience as she could imagine.

She said, "This seems like something from hundreds of years ago. Why paint it now?"

"Let me answer that," a voice said from within the throng of patrons. A woman wearing a mint-green silk toga and a crown of woven vines emerged and took Thomas's arm into her own. "After all, *I'm* the one who provoked you."

Thomas pecked the newcomer's cheek and said jovially, "Ash, please meet the peerless Lena Hänninen."

As Ash extended her hand, the other woman pulled her forward and wrapped her in a warm embrace. She could feel dense energy radiating in those places where their bare skin touched.

Lena released her and tilted her head toward the painting, saying with a smile, "My lovelies of the valley. I regret having to bid them farewell tonight, but alas, life goes on."

"What Lena means," Thomas said, "is that this *Divine Feminine* series is making her filthy rich. She paints, *we* bid. Rinse brush and repeat!"

Thomas and Lena laughed together for a moment, then Ash said, "You haven't answered my question yet. Why the old-fashioned style?"

"Because," Lena began, "there are more ways than one to resist the robots. And further—"

"Resist the robots!" Thomas declared in a booming baritone. "What a lovely turn of phrase. If someone would please procure for me a can of spray paint, I'll start the revolution out in the streets myself."

"What have *you* been drinking, my dear Mr. Templeton? Anyhow, as I was trying to tell Ash...

You don't always have to conjure up new *subjects*, when a fresh face or fanciful setting might also reveal great depths of insight. I don't care how many chess masters are humiliated by electronic opponents which can plot out a million hypothetical moves a second. No computer will ever peer into the history of its memory circuits in the way that people can examine their hearts and revisit some cherished memory from their youth—like the touch of fur at a petting zoo, or walking the beach boardwalk with their grandparents. Only we can sense these slivers from the distant past, and then decades later channel them into works of art that resonate deeply with people whom we will never meet—and were perhaps born long after our own lifetimes."

Ash said, "I think I follow you, but still don't see how you fit into this painting. Did you grow up on a farm?"

"No, and… you're maybe approaching this too literally. I paint in order to express my *perspective*."

"Which is?"

Lena grinned and rubbed her hands together. "Call it heresy, but I can't help but feel that all this new political power in women's hands is making us too cold. It's creating a different kind of callous, this being married to robotdom for twenty years. In my work I began to push backward, and through that process of exploration I ended up rediscovering the earthy femininity which had defined us for eons. So even if we can't actually return to the land—take a wild guess who does all the farming now—let's at least reacquaint ourselves with its sacred spirit."

Ash looked at the painting once again and was struck by the joyful and contended expressions on the women's faces. Despite their humble frocks and strenuous daily toil, they evoked a sense of harmonious living and true belonging. She glanced down at her own dazzling dress, and for just an instant felt self-conscious about having dolled herself up to make a big impression on this group of strangers.

"What are they singing about, in the painting?" she asked softly.

Lena said, "Those are Finnish farm girls. They pass the workaday hours singing traditional folk songs, which in turn keeps their cultural memories alive through voice and verse. Because, before jets and films started taking us anywhere and everywhere at will, people had real roots."

"The fact is," Thomas said conspiratorially, "that trees and vines and other creeping appendages all feature prominently in Lena's work. Some have even dared to suggest that these hold *phallic* connotations. The Green Man trying to have his way with Mother Earth, perhaps? But now we've heard the truth—our friend here remains pure of heart! Or so she says…"

"Listen to him," Lena admonished, "claiming to know so much about an artist's *real* intentions. If only we ladies were so bold as to presume his agenda. What do you think?"

Ash put on her best police officer's poker face and said diplomatically, "Maybe he's been eyeing your painting. Wants it for himself, but also hopes you'll be a cheap date."

"Oh, I wouldn't fall for that kind of flattery. It's certainly not *divine*. Well, sir, how do you plead?"

Thomas made as if to brush something away from his jacket sleeve, then said casually, "To be fair, I usually prefer my women in 3D rather than hanging on the wall. Something I can sink my teeth into."

"See?" Lena beamed. "I knew it all along. He

truly loves us!"

"Or he's gonna buy a sculpture instead," Ash said vaguely.

Lena gave Thomas a skeptical look. "Hmm, you might be right. But soon all will be revealed on the auction stage. So very nice to meet you, Ash. And as for you, Thomas, be sure not to pinch your pennies. Instead, cast them out generously and make all of our wishes come true."

As Lena stepped away, Ash pulled Thomas over to a table which had a selection of appetizers. They each loaded up a tiny plate and found a quiet place to eat.

She said, "I love how this is such an accepting group! 'Cause I was a little worried, earlier."

"About what?" Thomas asked, wiping his mouth with a small printed napkin as he chewed on a cocktail sausage.

"You know, me being a cop. I thought it might turn people off when they found out what I did."

"Do *I* really do anything? Hard to say. What does *work* even mean nowadays? Push a button... receive... consume... That's about it." Thomas smiled as he took another morsel from his plate.

"But still," Ash said. "I'm kind of a fish out of water here—I thought someone might call me out."

"Impostor!" Thomas pretended to shout while shaking his fist. Then, with a kind smile, "Not only would it be rude to put you on the spot, worse yet, the focus might turn back onto our own group of idlers who live outside of prescribed time."

"Ohhh, okay. So they're not too worried about the everyday stuff."

"We might be particular about the *things* we like, but otherwise try to treat people mildly. And we only panic when the flights we've booked are about to take off without us, haha. Now, in no uncertain terms will a dreamer ever be compelled to declare what they *do*. Creative miracles don't arrive in pre-packaged form, let alone on a set schedule, so patrons and artists alike must all wait for that next eruption of primal greatness. No one can predict when it will arrive, to whom it shall be granted, or what it will accomplish. That wild card is what we all find so exciting!"

Ash took a half step back and studied Thomas from head to toe. "Are you *sure* there isn't a bit of the artist trapped inside you trying to get out? Who knows, maybe these gallery nights will eventually push you over the edge…"

Thomas struck a noble pose as he said, "If only! But no, years ago those whimsical aspirations succumbed after being exposed to harsh, but irrefutable appraisal. Trust me, I do not have *it*."

"Awww, come here," Ash said, having seen his face take on a distant look ever so briefly. She gave him a firm squeeze, adding, "I was just having some fun. Didn't mean to bring you down."

"It's no bother," he said. "A little reverie about the paintings from my past might serve as a poignant reminder to always buoy the arts however I can."

"Ya know, *The Paintings from My Past* would make a great title. You could use it at the exhibition if your style got popular one day."

"More like, 'He spent so much money at the casino, we ought to cough up a few pieces of silver for the old check-writer.' In which case, of course, they would promptly toss those awful paintings into their attics. Good deed done, now good riddance!"

"Think you could show them to *me* sometime?" Ash cooed.

"Sounds like someone's angling for a trip to the islands," Thomas retorted. "If that's even where they're being stored. Would you still wish to see them if it meant a trip to New Hampshire at the height of winter?"

"Sure, why not? We can ski, light a fire, have a bottle of wine…"

"So you've got it all planned out? Interesting."

"Then I can tell people I knew you when—and inspired you to give that dream a second chance."

"Oh ho ho! Now she wants to play at being the muse! I must say, you do seem to be getting the hang of gallery life, yes indeed."

Ash moved in closer. She said, "I might even let you draw me. In the nude. *That* ought to get you reaching for your charcoal pencil."

"Or something else," Thomas said with a shiver.

"Now you're speaking *my* language, Mr. Templeton. My kind of canvas. My creative arts."

"And the exhibition?"

"By invitation only. Private showing—usually."

"Good lord… This is getting too scandalous, too —"

"*Hot.*"

"Yes, clearly. But if we keep this up, I'll risk missing out on the auction altogether."

"And why's that?" Ash said saucily, using her tongue to push out her right cheek.

"Be*cause*," Thomas said, pressing his thumbs down as he took hold of her shoulders, "I would be forced to ravish you like my less-refined ancestors once laid waste to entire continents."

Ash gasped. Her head swooned and she fell forward, resting her face on his chest with eyes closed. The gallery had ceased to exist. All she felt was her heavy eyelids as her breath moved in rhythm with Thomas's pounding heart.

Slowly, they came back down to earth. She tilted her face upward and felt his lips meet hers for a soft kiss.

"You mustn't work yourself up like that," he said with gentle concern. "We are writing our first symphony together. Each movement should progress carefully, deliberately, and *then* crescendo so that there can be no looking back."

"Yeah, to the climax. I understand all that, don't you worry!"

"Yessss, but… then *peace*. Instead of hunger for more."

"Oh." Ash felt herself plummet to the hollowest depths of agonizing loneliness. She whispered, "Like looking out the window while your lover sleeps…"

"Good heavens! We are taking you so far away —so far *ahead* of where this night is supposed to be. Let's go refresh our sensory palates on the patio."

As Thomas pushed open the wood-paneled glass door and Ash stepped outside, she breathed in the night air deeply. He plucked a small blue chrysanthemum from one of the potted plants and presented it to her. She savored the aroma, then watched as he threaded the stem through the lapel of his blazer.

"A claim check for later," he said, brushing a finger against the flower's edge. "And now that we have returned to our formerly austere selves, let's get ready to spend some money!"

Ash smiled and took his hand, and they went back inside the boisterous gallery.

6. THE STRAIN BEARERS

The man with the slicked-back hair Ash had earlier seen in conversation with Daphne and Stanley now ascended the stage. He smiled and brought his hands together as if in prayer.

"Hello, everyone. My name is Roger Vance and I oversee this gallery which you all have honored with your presence tonight. I wanted to take a brief moment to discuss why what we do here is so very special.

"The works of art we house at Muir Gallery, including those which will soon cycle through this room, represent success in a variety of ways. It requires a team effort to put on events like these, and as the captain I must acknowledge the dedicated staff who are my crew. With that being said, none would be possible without those creative power plants, the artists themselves!"

Roger paused and dipped a hand into his jacket pocket.

"Whereas almost anyone can be taught the

technical side of the creative professions, there is something absolutely unique about the internal makeup of true artists. They eschew comfort in pursuit of the magnificent. They possess the courage to forge daring new paths. But most significantly, they are the *strain bearers* who act as reflector... moral compass... and guiding light for civilization.

"And so tonight, we show our gratitude by offering their gifts to the world a loving home. Now, before we officially begin, I would like to invite the mother hen of Movement 24, Mrs. Carmella Edelweiss, to say a few words."

The audience clapped politely as the matron took the stage with a gracious smile.

"Creation is culture," she said. "Consumption is a choice. Therefore you must decide, will you ingest the immaculate or the indecent? My belief is this: art has been valued by all cultures because it is the primary *driver* of meaning, comprehension, growth, connection, and ultimately hope. To be able to relate to another person by way of a symphony or a painting, both unites and elevates us because it is *good.*

"Not every painting will be seen. Not every sculpture will survive. But every creator whose heart is clean and true, even if forgotten or lost to time, does in fact live forever. They are all soldiers in an army advancing inexhaustibly forward against the forces of doubt, darkness, and death. This is the spirit which endures, and it cannot be killed or replaced. Whether the land lies fallow or is built up to glorious heights, what matters most is that we keep alive the glorious spark that rises from humanity's depths."

Edelweiss looked directly into the eyes of several patrons as she moved across the stage and declared, "Only art is real. Even if you don't like what you see, you must appreciate when the artist has laid her soul bare. Meanwhile history, emotions, tales, and vows… all have the potential to wander off and become lies. *I* say it is better to disagree with one person's truth, than blindly swallow a popular falsehood.

"In turn, artists must not pretend… distract… obscure… or sensationalize their work. They must sign their name and stand by it. Even when we sometimes lose a feather," Carmella said as she smiled warmly at Marta Gionet, "we respect their choices while also reaffirming our own beliefs.

"I might conclude by adding that this aesthetic meiosis is why curators and critics also have such an important role to play. They are the great interpreters who pan for gold across the creative panoply. While it has been said that stability is the enemy of innovation, our complex ecosystem has devised a clever balance: some of us hold the calculator, so that the artist can focus on molding the clay.

"Let us now do our part to recognize that the battles waged in front of canvas and stone have been worthy struggles. Expression… which leads to appreciation… and finally *acquisition*. Bravo to all!"

The crowd cheered and Carmella Edelweiss was glowing with pride as she retook her seat. Moments later, a large door near the stage opened and the first lot was brought in.

Thomas Templeton rolled up his program and whacked it against his palm.

"And they're off!" he said to Ash with a satisfied smile.

A tiny oil painting of a covered bridge rested against the easel on stage. The auctioneer, a stocky woman with short gray hair, carefully straightened her charcoal blazer and then tapped her gavel.

The bidding started low, at only three thousand credits, but escalated quickly as five separate parties raised the stakes in rapid succession. Two of the bidders dropped out at twelve thousand. A third declined as the offer passed eighteen. The remaining pair flashed each other dirty looks in between offers.

Thomas kept his hand hidden behind the seat in front of him as he pointed toward the man with a paisley scarf tied around his neck. "That's Ernesto Ribisi," he whispered. "His family owns a winery in the Piedmont region, and their workforce is still one-quarter human. Someone once asked him why they didn't fully automate like most of the industry, and he quipped, 'You simply cannot replace the human foot.' Ha!"

"Sounds like a real character," Ash said. "And he flew all the way from Italy just for this?"

"Ernie is a serious collector. Expect to see him in the fray throughout the night."

"Now who's she?"

"Kendall Haines," Thomas said as they watched the woman in heavy white makeup and cream-colored fedora raise a gloved hand. Her eyes were hidden behind large black sunglasses. "She is the ultimate hoarder. Art, horses, ex-husbands, you name it…"

"Looks cold as ice to me. Who'd want to marry her?"

"Not I. But then again, Ms. Haines often gets what she wants. Perhaps one day I'll have no choice in the matter."

"Like what, she'll make you an offer you can't

refuse?"

"Imagine being presented with one of four mansions in which to live. And a wife who is rarely home. You could invite over any number of *younger* female guests to help cure your loneliness."

"I see." Ash clicked her tongue quietly.

"Thirty-two thousand, yes?" the auctioneer said.

Kendall Haines nodded gravely. The auctioneer turned toward Ernesto Ribisi, then said through compressed lips, "And thirty-five?"

The Italian waved a hand.

Up to forty, fifty, sixty thousand the bids soared. Murmurs rose from the crowd, and Thomas said, "All this for the first offering? We could be in for a record-setting night."

"Sixty-*eight* thousand, sir?"

As the auctioneer squinted in Ribisi's direction, he cast a disgusted glance at Haines before closing his eyes and shaking his head in resignation.

"Going once... twice... and sold to the gentlelady on my left for sixty-five thousand credits."

The gavel sounded, and the assembled crowd breathed a sigh as they clapped their hands. Event staff came forward to remove the painting from the dais.

"That was really exciting," Ash said.

"There's always high drama at this O.K. Corral," Thomas replied.

"Is your gun loaded?"

He shaped his hand into a pistol and aimed it at the ornate vase which was being staged up front. He said, "Listen for the shot. You'll know when it's me firing."

Ash subconsciously squeezed her purse. It held a tiny .380 pocket pistol which was tucked into a discreet padded sleeve. She was always ready to protect herself on first dates—because looks and bank statements could sometimes be deceiving.

"Fire away, pardner," she said. "I want *my* cowboy to win the day."

Thomas smiled and holstered the imaginary weapon on his hip. "Well, not at this piece. But soon, very soon."

The auctioneer retook her place on stage and the next round began.

7. THEY ALSO CARRY SHIELDS

"…going twice… last chance… going three times…"

The auctioneer lowered her gavel with a dull thud.

"No sale," she said curtly. "Perhaps another day."

As people began to whisper, the double doors slid open loudly and a petite man wearing a burgundy top hat entered the room. For a moment he looked toward the stage, then glared at the seated crowd before tugging at his lapels and storming off.

The chatter picked up, and Ash leaned close to Thomas as she said, "No sale. Does that mean his career's toast?"

"I wouldn't say that," Thomas replied, "but it *is* quite humiliating."

"What's he going to do? Throw a fit, or kill himself?"

"I presume Simeon is finding solace at the bar right now. Then he'll likely have a word with his agent—*someone's* got to take the blame."

"Blame? I may be new to all this, but even I know that art is up to the eye of the beholder. One bad showing can't be that big of a deal."

Thomas waved his program around as he said, "There are several ways in which to debut a new piece. Going straight to auction can be a bit of a gamble, but on the plus side, you create a sense of urgency which taps into people's covetousness. When done right there are multiple winners—the high bidder, the artist, and the various parties who all take their cut of the proceeds."

"But now?"

"They are all... losers." Thomas snapped his fingers. "Simeon bears the immediate brunt with all that egg on his face, but ultimately someone else will have to accept responsibility—for everyone's sake. Otherwise poor Simeon might not paint for months, and *he* is the cash cow. All the other links in the chain are expendable."

"If that's what was at stake," Ash pressed, "why didn't anyone just place a sympathy bid, or at least hire a ringer to do that?"

"Ashley, this is not a backroom card game. We have rules of honor here." Thomas cleared his throat. "No, this unfortunate and embarrassing episode is due to some sort of tactical error. Wrong venue, setting the opening bid too high, or the crowd's finicky tastes... any number of possibilities. And that *is* someone's fault, but not the artist's. All he's supposed to do—all he *can* do—is decorate the canvas."

"So what's next?"

"The show must go on! As you can see, the staff is now removing that orphan with the solemnity of pallbearers. If they could pinch their noses they would, haha, but they are wise and diplomatic enough to always play the long game. Simeon has made them money in the past, and surely he will shine again in the future."

"Ladies and gentlemen," the auctioneer began, "please retake your seats. Muir Gallery is proud to present the following item. It is lot number 8-D, as featured on page six of your brochure. *Erica the Waverider* by Yvonne Morrissey. Bidding will start at twelve thousand credits…"

"And here we go," Thomas said with a sly grin as he raised two fingers.

"You want this one?" Ash asked.

"Possibly."

"This should be interesting."

Ash eased back into her seat, glancing around the room to see who else seemed intent on bidding. After her detective's sharp eye spotted three other possibles, she turned her attention to the piece itself.

Mounted across two easels, this painting was six feet in length and three feet high. A stormy daytime sky merged with tumultuous seas. An overturned ship surrounded by wooden debris floated on the left side of the canvas. Approaching it from the right was a great mythical serpent, and standing atop the nape of its neck was a fearsome and voluptuous woman wearing ancient Roman battle leather. She was plucking helpless shipwreck victims out of the water and placing them down the length of the creature's back.

"Twenty-*six* thousand," she heard the auctioneer say crisply. "And eight. Thirty? Yes, we have thirty…"

Ash sensed Thomas adjusting his weight and looked over at him. His eyes were alert, moving back and forth from the painting to the auctioneer and the other bidders. Again he raised his hand.

"Forty-four…"

Who's his *Erica?* she wondered.

One of the bidders withdrew. Thomas raised to fifty thousand. Ash felt the surface of her body start to sizzle. She sat up straight, swiveling her head around like a periscope observing military combat.

Thomas suddenly dropped his shoulders. He folded his hands over the program in his lap, and shook his head with a delicate frown when the auctioneer turned to him with intent eyes.

The last two bidders continued exchanging fire.

"Eighty… I have eighty. Do I hear eighty-four? Eighty-two? Going once…"

The gavel sounded and a number of patrons applauded for the auction winner, who stood briefly to take a modest bow. Ash thought her head was going to explode.

"You didn't win!" she nearly hissed into Thomas's ear.

He pursed his lips and tilted his head ever so slightly.

"You didn't even fight…" she moaned.

Thomas reached into his shirt pocket and removed a folded kerchief. "For your face," he said.

Ash ran two fingertips along her hairline and felt the perspiration. She took the cloth and dabbed herself dry.

"Too hot?" Thomas said with a wink.

"You sly bastard. Was that all for show? To get me riled up, Mr. Rules of Honor?"

Thomas held up his palm in a gesture of peace. "A test run for me. And a welcome-to-our-world for you. Although I do appreciate Ms. Morrissey's talents, that particular series I'm not too fond of. I would only have purchased the painting as an investment, and fifty thousand was my limit."

"Erica's not your type?"

"I know what happens to the sailors she

rescues."

"Forced to join her private navy, are they?"

"No. *Used* first. Then killed... and finally eaten."

"Too realistic for you?"

"The ancient myths do appear to have become modern reality," Thomas said. "Sometimes a man must find a bastion of peaceful safety away from all the devouring Ericas of this world."

Ash didn't know whether to squirm or bite a chunk out of his left shoulder.

She said, "I'm starting to wonder... Maybe your knowledge of art doesn't carry over to reading the people you meet."

"Oh? How so?"

"You've... only seen me looking my best. Acting my best. And... well... I like you, Thomas. I really do. So understand me when I say, I might not show you any mercy if you ever see my own inner Erica."

He eyed her slowly. Blond hair blow-dried to a perfectly sculpted shape and flowing freely. Immaculate Swedish features enhanced by only the slightest hint of color and shadow. Freckled tan skin unsullied by ink or egregious piercings. Looking just as worthy as any other woman in the room.

"Now I'm beginning to see. You're the type of chameleon that blends in to prowl for fresh prey, rather than to hide. The goddess to whom all waters flow, because she is an end unto herself. And who perhaps knows no shame, in the belief that she cannot be defeated. Yes, I understand. You *want* me to charge forward madly and swing my sword at you."

"All night long," she purred.

"Well, it takes more to slay the dragon than by direct attack alone. Which is why all knights errant also carry shields."

"So I'm a dragon now? A sexy one, I hope."

"I could regale you with metaphors till dawn."

"Please do."

"You know," Thomas said breezily, "I *have* read Camille Paglia. I'm aware of just how much artistic expression down through the ages was each generation or culture grappling with the animal compulsion to sate its lusts. That will never go away, even if the consequences of the sexual act have been mitigated by technology—a sealed door here, a rerouted pipe there, and so forth. Maybe what the world yearns for today is another purpose… or function… or goal while playing with this primordial fire."

Ash exhaled through her lips slowly and fully. "And *you* came up with this theory all by yourself? That might be your big creative breakthrough right there."

"As my art, you mean? My great masterpiece?" Thomas thought for a moment, then added, "I suppose it's possible, but as you correctly stated, art remains in the eye of the beholder. Otherwise it risks the futile vanity of a tree falling alone in the forest."

"So you need me for… to do what, exactly?"

"You'll know very soon, I promise. Right after I win an auction."

8. TO KISS AND BE KISSED

"The next piece on offer will be *Loyalty's Treasures* by Samantha Minn. Please allow our staff five minutes and then the auction will begin."

Thomas pointed to the entrance of the prep room. A team of four was carefully bringing the giant walnut sculpture out toward the stage.

"Here it comes, your favorite!" he teased.

"Lemme see how much I got on me," Ash said, taking a moment to unzip her purse and peer inside. "Nope. I'll just have to sit this one out."

"Don't leave your seat though." Thomas craned his head around. "The room is really filling up now. I expect we'll see a spirited tussle involving several of the out-of-towners. *They* didn't leave their checkbooks at home."

After the piece was secured in place, the auctioneer rapped her gavel lightly and the people who were still standing took their seats.

"Thank you, everyone. Lot number Z-236 appears on page seventeen of your guides.

Composite acrylic exterior construction with mixed accoutrements. The year of design is 2045. Bidding will start at twenty thousand credits. Do I have a bid in that amount?"

Instantly a murmur spread through the crowd. Heads turned in mild confusion as the woman up front said, "Very good, sir. Twenty-two, anyone? Yes, thank you. And twenty-four now…"

"What's going on?" Ash whispered.

Thomas said, "Stanley Bennett has placed the first bid. I'd say that's a tad unorthodox."

"What's so weird about it?"

"He is one of Samantha's fellow artists. They don't usually buy each other's works at auction. Some might call it uncouth."

"I guess he's in a better mood now, at least."

"You might be right. Cooled his jets and is having some fun—or standing in solidarity with someone who *isn't* leaving the M-24 fold. I'll have to tell Sam about this little gesture, assuming no one else does first."

Ash looked around quickly while the auctioneer continued to tally the bids higher. "She's not here? I mean, she can't have gone home early?"

"Of course not," Thomas replied. "But no artist is ever present in the actual *room* when their work is being bandied over. You can't put extra pressure on prospective bidders, for one. And I doubt the artist's heart could bear that roller-coaster of a ride."

"Seventy-*six*," the auctioneer said crisply. "… and eighty… Yes, I have eighty-eight over there…"

"Well, good," Thomas said as he sat back in his chair. "Mr. Bennett is no longer in the running. One and done. So who's left… Ah, just as I expected. We have three of the usual suspects grappling for the honor of lugging that *nut case* back home."

Ash did a double-take. Slowly her face spread

into a smile she couldn't contain. "Thomas," she said, "you made another awful pun, didn't you?"

"Guilty as charged."

"Unbelievable! Oh well, that one was pretty good. And hey, I'm glad there's more to you than meets the eye, and you're not just some stuffed shirt."

Thomas pretended to adjust an invisible bow tie. "Word to the wise. Appearances often make the best smokescreens."

"Wait, are you really a government spy? And I'm your cover for some secret mission that's happening?"

"Drat, I've been found out! Yes, my assignment is to, um… make off with one of those hideous birds perched inside the walnut."

"…one hundred *fifty*," the auctioneer said with enthusiasm. "And sixty…"

Ash's eyes widened. She said, "I'm afraid you're on your own, Mr. Bond. If that thing sells for over two hundred grand, it'd be a serious offense to damage it."

"I was only kidding, of course," Thomas said. "No spycraft to speak of in my life. You as a detective are the closest connection I have to such matters."

Ash slid her arm through his as she said, "Tell me what you were doing at that gala again? My memory's foggy."

"Is it because you were so misty-eyed after our first encounter, or did that hunk of metal known as a bartender spike your drink?"

"Maybe a bit of both? Come on, be a good boy and tell Ashy."

"How shall I explain this?" Thomas said after a brief pause. "People in my sphere… at my altitude… Since we don't do anything remotely connected to work in the traditional sense of the word, it is imperative to maintain alliances. Therefore we make appearances, rub elbows—"

"And kiss ass?" Ash said, eyebrows raised.

"To kiss *and* be kissed, for the street runs both ways. There's a full schedule of dog-and-pony shows which ensures that none of us ever have to get our hands dirty."

Thomas presented his free hand and Ash inspected the cuticles. They were smooth, symmetrical, and without blemish. She quickly glanced at her own blue-painted nails, which one of the girls at Zuze's salon had hammered and buzz-sawed into presentability a day ago.

"Okay," she said, gently intertwining her fingers with his, "so you network. Arrange deals. Get awards with fancy dead people's names on them. Must be nice…"

"We *do* have to use our brains, you know," Thomas said. "Not everything in this world has been left to the Essential Planners—or the damned robots, for that matter."

"…two hundred thirty-five…" the auctioneer declared. "And forty now…"

Ash perked up again. The two remaining bidders were virtually sweating in the heat of battle—and Thomas's last remark had intrigued her.

"I didn't realize you were personally so anti-bot," she said. "I figured a man of leisure like yourself would take full advantage of anything that kept you from having to dig ditches."

Thomas said, "I can't tell if you're joking, probing for weakness, or what. So I'll say this. I am *not* here tonight simply to hobnob, or spend my money frivolously. I agree with almost everything that has been said by the others. Namely that real art, of the flesh-and-blood variety, is one of the last bastions where humankind retains its original purity of intention. I love how an imperfect brute can conjure something profound up from the depths, and then create a better version of *himself* during that mighty struggle to express the ultimate force."

"Sold!" Ash heard the auctioneer's voice proclaim. "Two hundred seventy thousand credits, to the gentlelady on my right."

As the seated patrons clapped once again, Ash looked at Thomas Templeton as if for the first time. "Who are you?" she said. "What is all this?"

He straightened his back and said, "As I have told you, I am merely a patron of the arts. Helping in my own small way to prevent this sacred corner from being smothered by all things safe, mundane, and *predictable*."

"And they really believe this, the other people here? It's not just an act?"

"Enough of them have their hearts in the right place, I'm sure. But like any scene that reaches a certain level of acclaim," Thomas added with a grin, "along with the spotlight come the pretenders, the hangers-on, and the know-it-all critics. If your bloodhound's nose hasn't sniffed them out already, you'll soon make their acquaintance in the celebratory afterglow following the last auction."

"Count me in. So what now?"

"At least no more of *that!*"

Thomas motioned to the front of the room, where *Loyalty's Treasures* was being painstakingly removed.

Ash laughed and gave him a pat on the chest. "You know, you're alright."

"Having fun?"

"Oh yeah."

9. DEFIANCE

Ash thought she had melted into a puddle of water down on the floor.

She could see her right hand holding the bulbous glass of red wine, knew that her right leg was crossed over the other. But she couldn't move, and the sounds of the room did not reach her mind.

She didn't even feel her heart anymore. It had begun to beat faster and faster until the massive thumping made her disbelieving eyes pulsate. And when the auctioneer said those fateful words —"Sold for three hundred and forty thousand credits. Congratulations, Mr. Templeton"—that was when she vaporized into this dissociated state. It was *beyond* anything she had ever experienced, whether physically, chemically, or verbally.

Watching Thomas wage war without words, let alone weapons, had transfixed her at first with curiosity and then mounting fear. How could a person remain seated and yet command so much power, simply by lifting a finger or nodding their head?

This was much different from when she herself played the part of the flirt, using coy glances to slowly draw someone in with tense magnetism. No, tonight Thomas Templeton had shown her *a new way*. Flattened her like moist, steaming asphalt under a ten-ton steamroller. Pitiless, inexorable, *purposeful*.

She twitched her head in his direction. "You did all that for... *to* me?" she gasped.

Thomas's slit eyes were cruel... triumphant... deeper with inscrutable mystery than any ocean the man-eating goddess Erica ever sailed upon. And Ash was wrecked—devastated and scrambling like some seaside village after being swamped by a flash flood.

"Three hundred thou..."

She trailed off and completed the unspoken thought in her mind.

I'm not worth it. No one is.

She heard Thomas sigh lazily and make a small sound. "Well, *that* was most certainly a spirited bout. And now I can enjoy the rest of the show as a spectator only."

This brought Ash back up off the floor. She gulped her wine reflexively, then suddenly realized she no longer had any idea what the item Thomas purchased even was. She glanced at the dais but it was empty. Two staffers were bringing the next lot in through the open door.

Sudden panic. Was it all in her imagination, or a gag? Had Thomas gotten Ash to implode her own mind through attitude and allusions alone, while he still remained at a zero balance?

"I want to see it," she said. "Up close."

"That's a wonderful idea. Just leave your program here and no one will take our seats now."

Ash composed herself and stood up, then managed to keep her balance without Thomas's offered assistance as they crossed the room. There was only so much humiliation she could endure in public, even if it went unnoticed because it was all in her head—and in every tense fiber of her body.

Because she and Thomas had both sat stock-still during that arms race of a bidding war, which as she now remembered pitted him against two other collectors. They had all vied recklessly while trying to possess the sculpture now standing before her in a small room off the back hallway.

It was a remarkable work carved out of dark green marble. A giant human hand was caught in the grip of some unknown beast's claws. There were signs of struggle, injury, strained muscles, and no clear victor.

"*Defiance*," Thomas said.

"Of the human spirit?" she asked.

"Hard to say, since we don't know who attacked first. But I find the title apropos, even if the backstory on this particular conflict remains shrouded. Not that being the aggressor necessarily makes one the guilty party, of course."

If she were younger, Ash might even have bitten her lip as she said weakly, "But… to pay so much?"

Thomas took her left wrist into his hands and made as if to check her pulse. "I get the rush too, believe me. It's not all theater, or the jet-setter's way of trying to impress their date. Truly, I love the piece."

"I think the old lady did too," Ash said, recalling the furious scowl one of the losing bidders had made after bowing out.

"All part of the game. The thrill of victory only takes you so far. You must also bear the sting of defeat from time to time. The *injustice* of it! 'How dare someone else triumph over me?' Oh, well. Tonight I'm the one who's singing."

Thomas laughed as he swiveled Ash toward the patio door.

"I do believe I've earned a cigarette, if you would be so kind as to join me."

"It's your party," she said with more admiration than she wanted to let on.

As Thomas steered her forward, Ash sensed that there had been a terrible mutiny at sea, and the goddess Erica, having lost control of her serpentine beast, was cast down into the raging waters. In that helpless moment, she didn't know whether to submit to the dominance of these chaotic forces... or begin plotting how she might reclaim her rightful command.

10. TOO GOOD TO BE TRUE

A roar went up after the auctioneer placed her gavel inside a velvet pouch and said, "Ladies and gentlemen, this concludes our showing. Thank you and good night."

In the mad scramble that followed, Ash shot up out of her chair along with everyone else and said to Thomas, "Time to hit the bars?"

He gave a bellowing laugh. "This crowd? Hardly! There might be some private after-parties later on, but the fun should really pick up here now that the tense part of the evening is finally over."

"Bring it on!"

Ash offered Thomas her arm and they sauntered out into the busy main room. A line had already formed near the bar, and as they took their place at the tail end Thomas said, "Just as I expected. Good thing I planned ahead."

He reached into his blazer and removed a silver flask.

"Whatcha got there?" Ash said.

"A taste of the islands. Rum from a boutique spirit maker back home. I know the owners. Would you care for some?"

"Gimme!"

Ash wiggled her fingers greedily and Thomas pulled the flask away.

"I'm not kidding," he said. "This is tip-top soup from a limited batch. So please, no glug, glug, glug. You must really savor it."

"Yes, Mr. Templeton."

Ash unscrewed the cap and poured a small amount onto her tongue. Instantly a sensation of rich spice caused her to rock back and close her eyes.

"Wow. That's... so good."

Thomas chuckled and eased the flask out of her grasp.

"And it's good to be alive," he said, taking an equally modest drink. "Good times with good company. I'm so glad you could make it out tonight."

"Me too. There's more going on in my town than I ever realized."

"And where do you normally get your kicks?"

Ash smiled demurely. That sip of rum might have warmed her tongue, but not enough to start revealing *those* secrets. After a few more drinks here at the bar, however...

"Maybe I'll show you sometime," she said, snaking a finger from the top of his chest down to his belt buckle.

"I'm counting on you to be my tour guide—I still don't know very many interesting places around the city."

"Ha! Be careful what you wish for."

"Was that a threat? If so, you must be sure to follow through."

She flashed her nails like a tiger about to strike. "I swear on these claws, you are hereby welcome to partake in the full Ash experience. Whether or not you make it through in one piece, that's up to you. But it won't be on *my* conscience."

"Death before dishonor, do you mean?" Thomas said.

"I dunno… You might have me confused with some other girl. I could get you into serious trouble."

"You? The lady who attended the same hoity-toity gala as all those other upstanding citizens and police administrators? Forgive me if I sound skeptical."

"Okay, just sayin'. I don't want you to be disappointed later. Or get hurt."

"Warning received. All I ask is that you don't bore me."

Ash put a hand on her hip, sticking the elbow out wide as she said, "Buster, where we're going, if you're bored it just means *you're* boring. Or scared."

"Fear doesn't win at cards or when acquiring art. So don't worry about *my* internal fortitude. Now, what shall we have to drink?"

"Still too early for a tequila shot?"

Thomas ever so lightly whacked the top of her hand. "Naughty, naughty! No, we are going to celebrate the new addition to my collection in style. Barkeep, that'll be two old-fashioneds, please."

"Cheers again," Ash said as they stepped away with their drinks. "How does it taste?"

Thomas, after clinking her glass, took a dainty sip and licked his lips like a lizard. He smiled. "We're in business."

"The relief I just saw on your face was

priceless."

"This beverage right here is why I believe in the power of… people power!"

"Are you feeling a little buzzed, Mr. Templeton?"

"And what of it? You're looking rather serene yourself."

"Feeling good, not gonna lie."

Thomas took Ash's free hand into his own. He said, "You… are beautiful. The most magnificent work of art in the entire house."

She brought his hand up and kissed it. "That's so sweet. This whole night is almost too good to be true."

"The very best."

As their lips touched for a second time, the intimate moment was broken when someone collided with them while rushing past. Before they could decide whether to protest or disregard the interruption altogether, they became aware of the larger commotion which had caused this person to behave so recklessly to begin with.

People were gathering noisily in an area where several of the auctioned pieces had been staged for celebratory photographs. Ash and Thomas approached as one painting in particular was surrounded.

Fingers pointed at the upper right corner—the space was no longer blank. It was red… blood red!

Ash let go of Thomas's hand, but hesitated as she made to reach into her purse for her police badge. Best to wait on that, she figured, not knowing what sort of pranks or other antics these M-24 devotees got up to on their big nights.

"This is outrageous!" one of the artists who had been signing autographs nearby shouted. "An affront to our integrity… our humanity! How dare they?"

Ash turned to Thomas, who had a bemused look on his face.

"What's going on?" she asked.

"This is curious," he said. "Stanley Bennett's canvas appears to have been vandalized."

"You mean scandalized!" a woman who was pressed close to them hissed. "Utter disrespect. Who would do such a thing—especially *here?*"

"Indeed," Thomas said while glancing around. "I see no questionable outsiders among this rabble. But someone must have a bone to pick with Stanley, good lord."

"Where is he?" Ash said. "And what's he gonna do when he finds out?"

"Normally, he would be within his rights to destroy the canvas. Or use a cleaning agent to restore the soiled portion to its original state, if he wanted. But since it has been sold, that decision rests with the new owner."

Just then, auction winner Principe Hahn arrived. He brought a hand to the top of his head and tugged at his hair, eyes blinking rapidly in bewilderment.

"Half a million credits, huh?" Ash couldn't stop herself from muttering.

"And he's getting every penny's worth," Thomas said with a chuckle.

"I don't know about that. He doesn't seem very happy."

"Oh no, he's absolutely loving this. The spotlight's on him now! Gets to put on his *own* artistic performance."

By now, Principe had calmed himself enough to speak. "Where's Stan?" he cried. "We must rally around him after this jealous insult—and then punish the coward who did it!"

"Here, here!" someone yelled in response.

The crowd dispersed and began calling Bennett's name as they went marching through the gallery. Some took the opportunity to pose for photos next to the defaced corner while affecting expressions of outrage and shock. Others gravitated to the bar.

"Ah, good idea," Thomas said. "Come quick. We must top off our glasses before the fireworks really begin."

"You don't have to twist *my* arm—or peel." Ash's eyes twinkled as she smiled up at him. "How mad do you think Stanley'll be?"

"I—"

A horrifying scream came from the back of the building. Ash instinctively set her drink down and hustled in that direction. As she made her way through the hallway which led to the gallery offices and private studios, she saw a cascade of nauseated faces turn away from the last door on the left.

Pushing her way past, she found Braxton O'Shea on his knees wailing over the motionless body of Stanley Bennett.

"Noooo!" he moaned. "It cannot be…"

I'll be damned. I knew something wasn't right.

Bennett was lying on his back. Some blood could be seen on the floor nearby. The shape of his throat was hideously deformed…

"Good God!" Thomas's voice came to her from behind. "Is this for real?"

Ash glanced back to see him slump against the doorframe, his expression forlorn and body sapped of all strength.

As other patrons who had been drawn by the uproar appeared beside him, Ash stood tall in front of the corpse and slid her purse zipper open. She retrieved her silver detective's badge, holding it high as she spoke.

"Ladies and gentlemen, your attention, please! A

terrible tragedy has taken place. And you are all witnesses. We need to lock this place down right now—nobody leaves until I've spoken to every last one of you."

"And who might you be?" someone whimpered from out in the hallway.

"Detective Westgard, JPC. This is *my* gallery now."

"But she's been drinking like a fish!" another woman griped. "I've seen her with a glass in her hand all night."

"Just do as she says," Braxton implored. "We have to find out what happened to poor Stanley."

"Damn right," Ash said. "Because one of *you* might be a killer. Someone better tell those caterers to brew up more coffee. It's gonna be a long night."

11. DEFENDING THEIR SANCTUARY

"Oh, no, you don't! Keep those godawful things out of here."

What now?

Ash walked toward the gallery entrance, where this latest crisis seemed to be unfolding. She found that several patrons were preventing a robot officer from entering. Little did they realize, or seem to care, how easily it could plow through them if its complex circuitry deemed them a threat.

"Hey!" she hollered. "What's going on here?"

Gallery director Roger Vance turned to face her, while also serving as a backstop for the resisting patrons. He said, "Did they *have* to send bots for this?"

"A lot of patrol units have 'em loaded in their trunks these days. What's the problem?"

"Ma'am, you've been here all evening. Surely you understand our philosophy by now. We simply *despise* robots, no matter if they wield a paintbrush, a weapon, or even a badge."

Ash quickly took stock of the situation—intoxicated creative types and their benefactors were becoming increasingly agitated, and had begun linking arms to defend their sanctuary. She would never get any useful information out of them if they were this uncooperative during questioning.

"Alright," she said to the director, "we'll keep 'em outside. But I don't want *anyone* thinking they can sneak off, guilty or not. So that's your responsibility. JPC won't be liable for what happens if one of those sentries has to chase somebody down."

"Understood," Roger said. "Thank you for the concession. Now, how may I be of assistance?"

"Let's get these people back inside, have them sit down somewhere."

As the patrons filed away from the doors after giving a victorious cheer, Ash stepped out into the warm night. A female officer she'd never met before approached.

"Hi Detective, I'm Carter. I take it the hardware needs to stay put?" The woman motioned toward the two bots that were standing nearby.

"Yeah," Ash said. "Got a weird bunch in there, but mostly harmless. Except for one."

"Dispatch mentioned you were here earlier as a civilian. Any idea who did it?"

"Not yet. I must've met half the people over the course of the night, but when you're not expecting anything to go down... Damn, do we really have to keep our guard up all the time?"

Officer Carter glanced away for a moment, then said, "Getting word that the cleanup crew will be inbound in five. Also, I'm pretty sure they've got a synthetic or two on board. That gonna be a problem?"

"I'll handle it. Thanks for the heads-up."

Before going back inside, Ash first went over to one of the JPC vehicles and fished out a blue parka. She threw it over her dress and then pulled her hair back into a neat bun.

The gallery atmosphere was somewhat calmer now, as the adrenaline rush of the past thirty minutes gave way to fear and concern. Most of the patrons sat huddled in small clusters on chairs that had been taken from the auction room.

Ash found the director in the back hallway, where he was speaking to the officer who had been posted outside the killing room to keep it secure and intact.

She said, "Mr. Vance, we need to talk."

The man smiled obsequiously. "Yes, of course."

"I got forensics landing any minute now."

"Certainly. Will they be removing... ?"

"Eventually. But the point is, that team's got bots, and there's no way they can process the crime scene as an incomplete unit."

"I see. Well... I know what to do. When they arrive, instruct them to enter through the rear of the building. I'll roll up the door."

"Works for me. After that's done, I'll need access to all of your footage from the event. Tech squad's gonna want it by morning."

The man sighed and raised a cautious finger. "Ah... about that. We... don't normally surveil our own private parties."

Ash and the other officer's eyes met briefly. She said, "Meaning what, exactly?"

"There *are* cameras installed throughout the facility, of course. With all the valuable works we house, it would be foolhardy not to have them. But on special nights like these, well, turning off the recordings serves as a preemptive Jubilee for all the human foibles that might otherwise end up in the permanent record."

"Are you telling me... there wasn't *one* camera on in the whole building?"

"I won't allow it!" the director sniffed. "This is our space, and our time. Where memories are made, hearts are opened, and the human spirit free to express itself without guile or calculation or fear. So yes, *that* is why I disable the electronic eye on auction night."

Roger Vance touched his heart and shuddered.

Ash said, "What about people's own devices? I know I saw some regular filming going on."

"Very true, but everyone expects that type of ground-level recording. It's the hovering menace which no one is equipped to be scrutinized by— where there isn't even one quiet corner for you to sneak away and enjoy an intimate moment."

"Uh-huh. Nothing quite so intimate as committing a cold-blooded murder after having lured your prey into that corner, maybe even *knowing* you were off the grid."

"Come now, Detective. *You're* human and on the police force, so I can't be the only one who still sees the merits of organic life."

"Yup. It's guys like you who keep gals like me in business."

Ash stepped away, and moments later received a video call from Chief Paraquez. The senior officer was at home, and appeared to have put on her uniform cap hastily, as it sat crookedly off to one side of her head.

"Hello, Detective Westgard," the chief said. "What kind of trouble are you stirring up tonight?"

"Right place, wrong time," Ash replied. "Spoiled a lot of people's fun, too."

"Even yours?" Paraquez lifted her chin slightly. "Nice dress, by the way."

"Thanks. And no, I didn't have mopping up after a murder on my dance card."

"Not the kind of *stiff* you were hoping for?" Paraquez's eyes flashed and a wine glass briefly came into view as she ducked down for a sip. "Okay, here's the deal. I'm tied up right now, so let me know everything you need to get the job done. I'll notify HQ to make any and all resources available, and after that the case feed will keep me in the loop on your progress."

Ash thought for a moment, then said, "I've got a lot of witnesses here, so anyone else you can spare to conduct interviews will help speed things up. I'll observe as much as I can, since I crossed paths with so many of these folks before all hell broke loose. Man, I really want to nail this SOB!"

"Otherwise, we know what our Sunday will look like."

"Yep. I guess I'll let you get back to… whatever you're doing. At least one of us is gonna have a good time, right?"

"Hey, chief or not, I'm still human. Just don't tell anybody!"

Paraquez winked and signed off.

12. CINDERELLA NIGHTMARE

Which one of you did it?

Ash scanned the gallery slowly. Along the walls her police colleagues were conducting interviews. Once completed, each patron would be herded over to a holding area in the auction room and kept separate from those still awaiting processing.

She had been hustling around in a supervisory role, but always on the lookout for anxious hands or eyes seeking a means of escape—anything which might tip off who the killer was.

Everything appeared to be under control and going smoothly. But this was *not* her forte. Pursuing leads, crawling into dark corners, and throwing elbows into an uncooperative perp's face—that was where Ash felt most at home. Not giving orders and actually having them followed to a T, when she herself so often broke with protocol after sensing that an investigation was losing precious time going by the book.

But now here she was, running an active crime

scene and playing the part, while her boss was the one out getting frisky. People were calling her *ma'am*. Responding to her every question and command with deference. It was a nice feeling, and a nice change of pace from that other type of respect which she sometimes had to enforce through violence…

She caught sight of Marta Gionet pacing nervously next to several others who were also standing around. The woman's expression was ghastly, as if she had aged decades in an hour.

A distraught Carmella Edelweiss put her arm around the young painter and said, "To lose not one, but two of my own on a single night? Surely you cannot leave me now!"

Marta wiped her eyes. "Forgive me, Carmella, but I must!"

"Oh dear, I think I might faint."

"Please, let me help you sit down…"

Ash approached the nearest officer that was on watch and indicated Marta Gionet as she said, "Keep an eye on her. Make sure she doesn't try to slip out."

"Understood. Will do."

Lena Hänninen was crouched along the wall weeping. Ash tried to muster a friendly smile as she walked past, but the stress of the moment and the thought that Lena might have killed Stanley Bennett herself made for an unconvincing effort.

Ash was slowly coming to grips with the depressing reality that her own Cinderella fantasy had turned into a nightmare for everyone. Despite still possessing both of her shoes and the clock only now about to strike midnight, she was back to scrubbing blood off the floors while the party guests eyed her with suspicion.

She felt her own heart grow cold and pitiless

toward them all, while her soul silently lamented that the wondrous dream had ended so abruptly. The hopeful seed that had sprouted within her during the early evening's warm glow, would now freeze and die during the harsh night of unfulfilled yearning...

The gallery was deathly quiet except for the muted voices of those being interviewed by Ash's colleagues. Both the party atmosphere and subsequent panic had completely drained away as the gravity of the situation sank in. It was a somber scene.

Ash saw Samantha Minn staring blankly into space, while the man sitting beside her rubbed her back and muttered to himself. One of the caterers approached with a small tray of coffees, but the man shook his head and the server moved on to another group.

Not far away, Braxton O'Shea was hunched forward in a chair nursing a disposable coffee cup. The woman on his left whispered into his ear while glancing around the room. Ash remembered that he had been one of the first to discover the body— mere coincidence or bold playacting by a murderer? Would Thomas tell her more about the man's character, or did secret ties among the wealthy supersede laws which they believed were meant only for the little people?

Suddenly Ash wished she was off the case entirely. Knowing all these people, no matter how superficially, actually put her at a disadvantage because her impressions of them were taking precedence over the raw facts. She didn't want *any* of them to be guilty, for her own sake as much as theirs. She didn't want Stanley Bennett to be dead, either. Because if something so terrible could happen at an art gallery, then maybe no corner of the world was safe from the horrors which were Ash's stock-in-trade.

The glittering majesty of this night had been extinguished irrevocably. Now all that was left for her to do was trudge forward with her mop and fulfill the sworn duties of a police officer. There was honor in that, at least.

"Oh my god," she whispered. "I already blew it."

Ash realized with painful clarity that there could be only two possibilities—either the murderer had quietly left the gallery immediately after committing the crime, or had only stayed because they were confident of not being found out. Meaning that all of these urgent witness interviews were unlikely to secure a confession, because the killer was already long gone or had performed so flawlessly that Stanley Bennett's death was their own work of inscrutable art.

The gallery director had made it abundantly clear to Ash that there was no proper surveillance video, but perhaps someone on staff had done a formal headcount earlier in the night. How many people had gone home early? She supposed the tally could also be pieced together by the tech team when it scoured through whatever sparse footage was collected from the patrons' own personal devices.

Even more concerning was the notion that if the patrons themselves had also mirrored the gallery's policy by not filming each other surreptitiously, then this material might be of little value to the overall investigation. The bulky antiquated devices Ash had seen people using to snap candid photos throughout the night now made more sense.

But wait!

Regardless of whether or not the building's own outdoor cameras had been disabled for the duration of the event, any number of cameras mounted on the street lights and surrounding structures would still have been operational. If the killer had indeed fled, surely this footage might help identify them, even supposing that some of the other attendees also departed around the same time.

Ash quickly keyed instructions to the police department's tech team about the importance of obtaining this other footage, then turned her attention back to the task at hand: dozens of guests still needed to be processed, and one of them might turn out to be Stanley Bennett's killer.

Where are you?

She circled the gallery once more. With compressed lips and hands clasped behind her back, Ash gave everyone she passed a hard look—a pitiless laser beam that cut through all artifice and mortified those who earlier had exchanged carefree banter with Thomas's new friend, the pretty blond named Ashley. Now they recoiled from her with equal parts fear and revulsion, because she had transformed from potential princess into a blue-collar grunt getting her hands dirty with something other than paint or clay.

And in turn, it was *Detective Westgard* who felt disdain for these denizens of society's most frivolous class, as well as the court jesters plying their obscenely priced wares.

And yet…

She caught a glimpse of the back of Thomas's head and held her breath. Why should she lord over these people who, however pretentious or buffoonish, were almost all innocent of murder? She had no right to mock or humiliate them, and now regretted making a show of her superiority simply because the opportunity had presented itself, when for hours she had aspired to be their equal.

The truth was that until a short while ago, Ash had also been thinking pleasant thoughts about sleeping with Thomas for the first time. The where, the how... but then in a flash, an unforeseen event had turned this playground for the wealthy into her own sandbox—and she could already feel the worst aspects of her own personality rising to the surface. Ego. Dominance. Impatience. Callousness. Where even justice for a murder victim might be polluted after she used it as a steppingstone for her own ambitions.

Had she known in her heart that an elegant new dress couldn't possibly bridge the gap, when it was still Ash the resentful outsider wearing it? All night she had wanted so badly to indulge the temptation to let down her guard, let her anger fall away, and so much more...

But it was not meant to be.

She looked up at the ceiling and exhaled fully, then thumped a hand hard against her hip.

I'm gonna catch this bastard. For ruining everyone's *night.*

13. BROKEN BEHIND THE SMILES

As she continued to zigzag through the gallery, Ash heard a man say, "It's like he was being hounded, and painting wasn't enough. So he hounded everyone else, too."

"Mm-hmm," replied a tall and slender woman whose black ponytail was accented by gray strands. "Always running at full capacity."

"He couldn't help himself."

"Still, people need room to breathe."

"Someone got fed up with him, that's for damn sure." The man shook his head. "But what's a guy like Stan supposed to do? He had a message to spread and the talent to do it."

The woman looked down at the top of her hand and said, "Maybe the real reason they killed Jesus was for being so pushy. *He* wouldn't let people ease into the new gospel, either."

"Come on," her companion said with a laugh. "Who's ever allowed to just *ease* into a revelation— or a revolution—on their own time? We certainly weren't twenty years ago."

"I suppose you're right. But now it's artists playing the martyr, instead of just painting them like in the past."

"And if Stan was overturning the cash registers in *this* temple, maybe someone felt threatened enough to think he had to be stopped."

The woman pursed her lips, then said, "How many times did he accuse someone else of being a phony, or scared of greatness? Idealistic tough talk like that only gets you so far—especially when Universal Basic Everything gives people the *illusion* that their needs are being met. But still, you can't program success."

"Or approval from your peers," the man added. "I'm telling you, he just never saw the big picture about how it all works."

"Or people."

The pair finally sensed Ash's presence and slowly moved away.

She began racking her brain trying to remember all the times she had seen Stanley Bennett throughout the night. Like everyone else he had been jumping from group to group, and Ash hoped that she might have subconsciously noticed something which could help her now.

Beyond that dramatic scene with Marta Gionet early on, as well as her own personal conversation with him, Ash had at one point seen Bennett gesturing wildly while speaking to Carmella Edelweiss. Then later, he and another man passed behind her while talking loudly, but she didn't know where they'd gone or what they were discussing.

During the nearly three-hour auction, Ash only saw him briefly. He hung around for a few of the early offerings, but only placed the one bid before stepping away. She hadn't thought to ask Thomas where the artists went to sweat out those nerve-racking moments while their works were up on the block.

She was convinced that in such a packed venue, there must have been someone else besides the killer who had interacted with Stanley in the moments leading up to his death—and any small detail they remembered might help identify who was lying in wait. Ash quietly typed a message instructing the interviewers to add this specific item to their list of questions.

Thinking back on the half-hour window between the last auction ending and Bennett's body being found, Ash had to admit that by this time she was feeling a bit tipsy. Her mind was at ease and drifting toward a lovely place, when that first dreadful cry wrenched her back to gritty reality.

She was wide awake now, and watching everyone like a hawk.

The smell of freshly brewed coffee drew her toward the catering station, where the four waitstaff had been doing yeoman's work loading up trays and delivering drinks to the huddled guests. She was only ten feet away when Kendall Haines came up to her with a look of annoyance on her face.

"So you're in charge here?"

"I am," Ash replied. "The name's Detective Westgard."

"Nice getup." Haines flicked a finger at Ash's windbreaker-and-dress combo. "Very 2010s. Now look, I'm ready to pick up my painting and get going. Think you can manage that, sweetie?"

Ash couldn't believe her ears. If she were able to get away with it, she would have gladly smacked this shrew across the face—but there were far too many people around for that. Instead she said, "You must be joking. A man is dead, last I checked."

Kendall waved her hand. "I don't own any of Bennett's works. Why should this involve me?"

"Ms. Haines, ma'am—"

"Oh, so you know me and still won't budge? I'd like to speak to your supervisor."

"I heard your name earlier, okay? But I'm the boss here, so..." Ash leaned close to the woman's ear. "If you don't want to be put under arrest for interfering with a criminal investigation, I suggest you sit down over there and keep quiet."

Kendall Haines turned up her nose and gave Ash a dismissive glance, then went stomping over to the bar.

"Martini with extra olives, let's go," she said with a snap of her fingers.

"I apologize," the caterer replied, "but we were told to stop serving alcohol. There's juice, water, coffee, tea..."

"But I need something for my nerves!"

Ash decided to step in. She tapped the JPC logo on her parka, then whispered to the woman tending bar, "Pour a bit of whiskey in her coffee. You have my permission."

"*Thank you*, Detective," Haines said as her drink was being spiked surreptitiously. "I just knew we could get along. I'll be right over there waiting for you to say when it's time to leave."

"Great to hear. Enjoy your coffee."

"Oh, I will!"

Ash turned back to the caterer and said, "Hi again. Pour me one as well, please."

"Sure thing. Cream, sugar... whiskey?"

"No, no. Black is fine." Ash received the steaming cup and said, "Now I see why the director insists on having real people pour the drinks."

The woman smiled. She was in her late thirties and wearing a uniform of white dress shirt and black polyester slacks. With a slight twang in her voice she said, "Boss knows we're a dying breed. We all work other gigs anyhow. But this is fun, gets you out of your head and into whatever action's going on at the time."

"I see." Ash took a sip of her coffee. "Mm, this is good stuff. So tell me, uh…"

"Natalie."

"Tell me, Natalie, since we can probably cross you off the list of potential suspects—did you see anything suspicious from your vantage point here behind the bar?"

Natalie shook her head mildly. "There's no time to look around. Every five seconds someone else wants a drink, or two. Mix, pour, open a bottle, refill the ice tray… Sometimes I barely *see* the person I'm serving."

Ash scratched at the side of her cup. "What about your ears? I'm not saying you eavesdrop, but maybe you happen to pick up some of the chatter going on around you?"

"I mean… One of the reasons they hire us is to be discreet. People can practice selective hearing. Robots, maybe not so much."

"Yeah, I follow you. But in one of those back rooms, a star from tonight's show lost his life. Now I'm wondering, was this a crime of passion or the first strike by some anti-art serial killer? We don't really know anything, which is why even some random whisper in the back of your mind might actually be significant."

Natalie placed her hands wide on the bar top, closing her eyes as she bobbed her head.

"I'm thinking," she said. "Trying to hear it all again. There were a lot of strong *opinions* in the air tonight."

"Love or hate for the works on display?" Ash

said quietly, having leaned in closer.

"There's always some of that on auction night. People get themselves worked up, like they're betting on a favorite horse. No, the tone was more bitter... almost annoyed... Like you could tell something was broken behind the smiles."

Natalie finally opened her eyes and nodded firmly.

"That's it," she said. "Some people aren't happy about the changes going on with the scene, now that it's starting to get attention."

Ash set her drink down. She said, "Okay, now we're getting somewhere. Sounds like you're talking about rivalries, infighting, that type of thing. Were any specific names mentioned?"

"Ma'am, these nights I tend bar are a blur. What I'm telling you now is like a summary, the general theme of what I heard over the course of hours."

"Then tell me this. Was all the trash-talk one-sided, or did some people try to defend whoever was being criticized?"

"Oh, yeah! They were going at it back and forth. Because you're not gonna pay eighty or ninety thousand for a one-off piece, and then let someone in a pink bow tie knock it without speaking up, right?"

"Ah, so you *do* you notice things with your eyes."

Natalie smiled briefly. "Yeah, maybe. Bow tie guy left me a nice tip. I don't remember if *he* actually said anything about the art, if you know what I mean."

"Of course. And some of these collectors fly in from all over. I'm sure it's very exciting for them. Hmm. Are you absolutely sure this isn't just a normal part of the ritual?"

"Officer, there's something off about these

people in a way that wasn't before. Did I expect a guy to get killed? No. But now that it's happened… I'm still shocked, but maybe it was inevitable."

Ash's mind was racing. How well did this barmaid really understand the art world's inner workings?

She said, "I don't know what to make of you. You're laid back one minute, but then casually dish out what some might call inside information. What do you *actually* think?"

Natalie looked Ash directly in the eyes. She said, "I've been a musician since I was twelve years old. Played in a lot of bands and ensembles that never went anywhere. Blame it on lack of chemistry, bad timing, different overall visions, whatever. Usually the split is friendly enough, because we're all just little fish trying to find our way. Do you follow me so far?"

"Go on."

"But when a group locks in and starts to get some recognition, that taste of power can be very tempting. If you stop seeing eye to eye from up there, the term 'irreconcilable differences' comes into play. And if you still can't make peace for the sake of the big picture—to preserve what you already built—then it's separate or die."

Ash could sense a subtle change in and around Natalie's eyes. The woman was looking at something far away which seemed to affect her deeply.

"You don't really wanna be a bartender, do you? You had another thing going that was much bigger."

Natalie sighed. "I sure did. But hey, at least I'm alive, right?"

"I do hope you're still playing… or singing. Doing whatever it is you're good at. Maybe another band will come along."

"Maybe. But you don't always have to *die* to lose the spark. Blind hope is what fuels all those manic hours it takes to turn an idea in your head into something larger than life."

"I'm not all that creative," Ash said. "Sorry if I don't understand what you mean."

"Most people," Natalie said as she brought her hand down in a forward chop, "they just plow ahead steady like a mule. Players, on the other hand, can be volatile. There's deposits of chaos buried in the soil we tap into. But... it's not infinite. We can't squeeze the sponge forever. Can't always just *give*. We also need to be replenished and sustained. That's what these nights at the gallery are supposed to be about."

"For you?" Ash said gently.

"Yeah, I guess I feed off the energy. Try to siphon some of that belief over to my own tank. Because I only have enough left for one last go, and right now... Think I'd rather keep it inside and not risk burning it off on a losing gamble. Otherwise I'd know for the rest of my life, it was really over."

"Thank you sharing that. Please don't give up."

Natalie topped off Ash's coffee.

She said, "I bet you'll find that everyone you talk to here has *heart*. And as for your killer? Maybe they won't turn out to be so *evil* after all."

"And instead, what? Just unable to *reconcile* their emotions?"

"Isn't that what art, and life, are all about?"

14. THE ULTIMATE CURATOR

Ash figured she ought to check in on Thomas. He wasn't exempt from the interview process, and prudence meant that she would not observe his Q&A session.

She found him seated in a small circle of guests. He scooted his chair around to face her, then rose as he took her hand gently.

"This has been quite the first date," she said, allowing her fingers to intertwine with his.

"Just the sort of thing I had in mind. *Memorable*." He gave a wry smile.

"I guess now you'll get to know the real me. Hope it doesn't freak you out."

"Oh, I've been watching you out of the corner of my eye. Very impressive, the way you marshal everyone around."

"Doing the best I can. So how are you holding up? I seem to remember you and Stanley having a few laughs together earlier—how well did you two know each other?"

Thomas rubbed his forehead for a moment, then exhaled. "Stan was the real deal, and I admired him greatly. Anyone who can set aside their own ego for five minutes will admit as much. And now? Cut down long before ever reaching his major-works phase. It's an absolute tragedy. The world has been robbed."

Ash said, "So… it was more appreciation on your part than actual friendship? Not that I'm saying you weren't genuine or anything…"

"Ha!" Thomas said almost too loudly. He then added, "This world I've dropped you into is the ultimate mutual-barnacle society. We all need each other, so we all feed each other. Money, praise, access, whatever it takes."

"And you knew Stanley going back how long?"

"Am I being formally questioned now?"

Ash stepped in close. She said, "Come on, you know I'm your alibi—the best in the house, too. I'm just trying to get a better grasp of all these dynamics. Plus, the sooner I catch the killer," she whispered huskily, "the sooner I get to *grasp* something else."

Thomas contemplated her for a moment. "Incredible. You are a human avalanche. And I suppose no one ever escapes your path?"

Ash shrugged her shoulders. "About Stanley?"

"Yes, of course. I must have met him four or five years ago in passing at some to-do. It was in Switzerland, if I'm not mistaken. Whether he was on his own or funded by a benefactor at the time, I don't recall. But he was everything then, that you also saw tonight—impassioned, philosophical, full of righteous sound and fury. But here's the crucial point: his great talent in life was actually being realized, unlike so many others who squander their inborn potential. His heart was always in the right place, so how could we not forgive him his exuberance?"

"Did you buy any of his paintings? 'Cause if you did, seems like they're gonna skyrocket in value."

"That is a cold thing to say, Detective." Thomas put his hands into his pants pockets and looked away.

"I'm sorry." Ash touched his back briefly. "I was only thinking out loud. My mind is racing a mile a minute trying to piece everything together. I didn't mean to insult you."

"Apology accepted. And to answer your question, no, I was not a patron. We can't support them all. However, Stan did once give me an early sketch of a nature scene he had painted. Artists will make gestures like that, just so you know. To acknowledge their sincerest supporters by presenting them with a memento that the world doesn't even know exists. I shall cherish it even more now."

Ash glanced at the gallery entrance and sighed. The latest JPC reinforcements had arrived.

"I have to get back to it," she said. "But just a head's up. When you're being questioned, keep it simple. *They* don't need to know all the nuances of this art stuff. Their only goal is to trip people up, so don't take the bait."

"That's all well and good," Thomas said, "assuming they're not as relentless as you." He smiled at her kindly.

"Ha, yourself. No one is. See you in a while, Mr. Templeton."

As Ash reluctantly stepped away to greet the officers who would help expedite the interview process, she wondered why Thomas should elicit such *humane* thoughts in her. It wasn't her style at all. Too often she merely pretended to lose herself, so that the other person would be caught off guard when she turned the tables on them later, either by taking control or taking off completely.

Ash began to sense that she was actually in the middle of a duel, squaring off against a unique and worthy rival in the person of Thomas Templeton. He had invited her into his own lair and was running laps around her, until the discovery of a lifeless body suddenly changed her fortunes.

Thomas had become just another anxious face in the crowd. All those delicate people with quivering lips, pleading for Ash and her no-nonsense crew to assure them that everything would be okay. They were helpless until the killer hiding in their midst was apprehended, and only then could they hope to return to their pompous and granular pursuits.

Christ, I am so heartless.

Ash was mad now. First, at her own mind for spinning yarns out of hypothetical scenarios. And also at the whole situation, when at this very moment she could have been extracting the naked truth from Thomas herself. She was determined to find out what species of night beast hid behind those infuriating boat shoes he wore, his collection of rustic cable-knit sweaters, and his closets full of silky slacks with impossibly perfect pleats...

But none of that fancy stage dressing mattered after the lights went down. Refinement was nothing but a vulnerability on Ash's rolling deck, as massive waves from the Earth Mother's ancient depths surged forth to shatter all the trappings of decorum into a thousand pieces of flotsam and jetsam.

It was Erica the Devourer come to life. The everywoman whose mere presence whipped men into the kind of frenzy that started wars and inspired boundless creativity. Incalculable effort expended throughout human history, just so that she might smile approvingly upon he who had ground himself into dust through bloody combat, or while trying to unlock nature's secrets.

All of this was done to please *her*, and gain access to her body…

But what no one ever seemed to perceive, let alone grasp, was the burden of being that judge. The strain of looking out at that endless procession which wound its way off into the distance, as each suitor eagerly awaited the chance to present his own offering with plaintive doe eyes. You simply couldn't reward them all.

And then came the rising doubts…

The creeping suspicion that this tribute was made more in the name of a *concept*, than you personally. Next you began to wonder if you were even worthy of this task. How many times had you chosen wrong? How many worthy men had you doomed to obscurity through your own apathy, insolence, and ignorance—and thus stunted the future of the entire world?

The implications were staggering…

Crushed under the weight of an imposed responsibility whose powers you were never trained to utilize or exercise properly, you not only sensed, but *knew* it had all been a horribly cruel distraction, which in turn denied *you* the chance to fulfill the potential of your own personal destiny.

No, the world never did understand why the goddess might possibly be unhappy. It did not see that this role of appraiser tore her mind and heart in every direction, until she finally broke down exhausted and paralyzed in a tangled knot.

Hysterical, they would say. Hormonal. Weak. Unfit for command.

Even now, when half a million Ericas served as auxiliaries for the Essential Planners who oversaw the mechanized worldwide build-out and cleanup project, the old tropes persisted through impolite banter which cut like a knife. As if the species itself remained unwilling to accept that Erica could be more than a womb, more than a whore... that there was more to her identity than being the world's ultimate curator... and she could truly be whatever it was she wanted.

Even a cop.

This thought brought Ash back to reality. But she was still floating, now just a pair of eyes darting around the room taking stock of all these *self-appointed* curators. Some of them had even participated in the bidding war for that Erica painting—the piece which Thomas had pretended to want while toying with her emotions. To twist her around and knock her off-balance. To make her doubt herself.

So that now, despite these last two hours which she had spent in full control, Ash knew she was worse off than before. Worse than ever. *Ever.*

She didn't know how she was going to make it through the night. A killer was idling some twenty or thirty feet away, while a prospective lover also sat nearby. Meanwhile, she had gotten herself lost trying to solve the riddle of female existence, which had confounded poets and painters and philosophers alike since the dawn of time.

What the hell is going on?!

Detective Ashley Westgard ran a thumb over the contours of her police badge. She needed to *solve* this murder quick. Her heart, her body, her soul, and the struggles of humanity itself would all have to wait.

15. THE TOWER

During a brief lull while all of her team members were occupied, Ash decided to give Stanley Bennett's painting a closer inspection.

It had been roped off as part of the crime scene, and she now slipped past the cop who was standing guard. The other works nearby had been moved into a semicircle, each standing silent and triumphant after the lucrative battles waged to obtain them.

Ash approached *The Tower*. Bennett's final public work. "Magnificent," a woman seated beside her had remarked when it was unveiled on the auction stage. Indeed, it *was* striking up close. Even Ash in her relative ignorance about aesthetics could recognize the quality and its similarities to the Impressionist style.

Her eyes were drawn to the rising spire in the center of the canvas. It was thickly rendered with whitish curving brushstrokes, a cylindrical tornado surrounded by the faint blue sky which extended past the upper edge.

Down below a chaotic scene of small human figures was playing out. Some were running away from the spire… others kneeling in supplication near its base… and one group was even doing battle with machetes and clubs.

Off to the sides, life was proceeding as normal. There was a bustling outdoor cafe. Laborers tending to a field. Rowboats full of fishermen in the bottom right.

Ash glanced up—there was that egregious dark red stain across the top corner. Stanley Bennett's blood, which had been used to "complete" the picture.

She wondered about the motivation behind this insult. Killing Stanley alone in a secluded room, where the din of the festivities might drown out any dying screams, was far less of a gamble than defacing the canvas so brazenly.

Surely the performance of this symbolic act had been as important to the murderer as delivering the fatal blow itself. But to what end? Desecrate the painting because it was an extension of Bennett's body and soul? Or as a rebuke against M-24's trademark, the intentionally abandoned work? But again, in order to say what?

Perhaps the killer simply had a violent temper. Maybe he or she was already known for making threats against other artists. Or had a ghost from Stanley Bennett's past come back to haunt him?

Turning her thoughts back to logistics, Ash inspected the bloody smear with an eye for how it might have been applied. It was thin, a quick swipe from left to right, as if the killer had done the deed in haste.

She couldn't believe that this person would have dared to casually stroll through the gallery with a bloody hand that might drip and leave an incriminating trail along the floor. So there must have been something absorbent, like a handkerchief or paper towel, which could be hidden and relied upon to stain the canvas's blank space at the crucial moment. Then it would need to be disposed of quickly... and permanently.

Ash made a beeline for the restrooms in the back hallway.

In total there were four private compartments, as she remembered from her one trip there earlier in the night. Each was equipped with a urinal, traditional bowl, and wash basin. Her gut said that the bloodstained accessory must have been flushed down one of the four bowls—but how many times had *those* been used by patrons waiting to be interviewed during the past several hours? Traces of potential evidence first being contaminated by bodily fluids, and then flooded with high-pressure water surges over and over... The thought made her sick.

Now everyone would have to hold their bladders, because until the forensics unit conducted a comprehensive analysis, these facilities were off-limits.

Ash felt some of the tension ease from her body. Somehow the blind maze of her thoughts had led to a possible breakthrough, and the time had come to act decisively.

While forensics scoured the bathrooms for blood traces, she would instruct tech to refine its study of the collected handheld footage by focusing on two specific details. First, by isolating the twenty-minute window surrounding the estimated time of death. And second, tracing the path which led from the killing room out to the easel in the main gallery, and then back to the toilets.

Just maybe, they would get lucky and see

someone moving urgently along this route. But if the results came back inconclusive, then solving the murder might boil down to old-fashioned police work—which meant real-time electronic surveillance of the hundred-plus auction attendees, as well as going through their backgrounds with a fine-toothed comb. A lot of private lives were about to be pried open unceremoniously.

As she beckoned an idling officer to stand post outside the restrooms, Ash wondered what biographical details about Thomas Templeton might come to light… and if she was willing to risk endangering their chances of success by glancing at that cheat sheet.

As dawn broke and the last of the interviews concluded without any significant breaks in the case, Ash knew it was time to formally hand the reins over to Chief Paraquez. Her own little experiment in crime scene management hadn't been a disaster, not by any stretch, but apparently the big win she'd wanted wasn't in the cards. The identity of Stanley Bennett's killer remained a mystery.

Thomas was among the first groups to be released, and Ash went to see him off.

"I must say," he said jovially while adjusting his wool driving cap, "this has been quite the operation. Efficient work by all involved."

"Thanks. I hate to be sending you home alone, but I'm completely swamped." She gave his hand a quick squeeze. "Truth is, I don't usually have this kind of responsibility."

"Could've fooled me! You seem to be completely in your element. And I, for one, am glad not to be the killer, because surely I would have cracked in this stressful environment. But tell me, do you have any hunches or leads?"

"Unfortunately not," Ash said, keeping her voice low so that no one else would hear this admission. "Whoever did it hasn't blinked so far. And now I've got to let them all go. Feels like I should've done more."

"Oh, hush. You're with the Corps for a reason. I have every confidence that after a committed team effort, justice will be done."

"Let's hope so. And FYI, everyone here is gonna be tracked for a while—even you, so be prepared. But damn! I was really holding out hope that we'd put cuffs on someone before morning."

"What, and get all the acclaim for yourself?"

Thomas raised a placating hand before Ash could respond.

"Oh yes," he said, "I understand very well. You too possess some of that heroic spirit we've seen on display here in the gallery. I gathered that right from the start."

"Yeah?" Ash cracked a smile. "I'm flattered you think so. Although… I was more interested in getting back to our date than reading any news stories about myself."

Thomas removed the blue flower from his jacket lapel and placed it into the palm of her hand.

"Remember, good things come to those who wait."

"Even bad girls?" she said playfully.

"*Especially* them. So get back to it. Farewell, Detective… we shall meet again!"

Thomas walked through the open sliding doors and sauntered out into the early morning haze.

The doors closed and reflected an image of Ash back to herself. In the five seconds of peace she had before another patron blocked her view while asking a question, she knew that she had felt something. But what?

Emptiness? Longing? Relief? As she absently put the flower inside her purse, Ash could only describe the sensation as being... *not-Thomas.*

The evasive enigma she'd finally gotten out on a date. The dance partner who led with a firm hand, but never failed to treat her with respect. And later on, the bystander who had watched her work with keen interest.

Now he was gone. Off to wherever he stayed in town. Off to do whatever a man who could afford to drop mini-fortunes did on Sundays. Not that days of the week made much difference to people from his station in life...

And yet, even after the disappointment of how this night had played out, Ash couldn't help but wonder if she still might breathe in that rarefied air one day—and all the sooner should she be the one to find Stanley Bennett's killer. This tempting prospect was motivation enough to keep her powering through the job without any sleep.

Once she got the gallery cleared out, Ash would run home quickly to shower and change before meeting with Chief Paraquez and the homicide squad to make a battle plan for day two of the investigation.

Then she would be just another cop working the case. No more having people defer to her. Nobody at her beck and call. But also, no one looking over her shoulder.

Thus untethered, the real Detective Ash would be free to do what she did best—unleash hell in the name of justice.

16. DOGCATCHERS

"Alright, team. Let's get into this."

Chief of Detectives Gabriela Paraquez stood alone at the front of the briefing room. She gripped the edges of the podium and consulted her notes.

"The victim: twenty-eight-year-old Stanley Bennett. Professional artist. Killed last night at Muir Gallery during an event that was attended by over one hundred people, including our own Detective Westgard. Time of death, shortly after ten pm. He was found strangled in one of the back rooms after the auctions had concluded. In addition to the severe damage to his throat and neck, Mr. Bennett also incurred a laceration on the left side of his head. The cause of that is still pending lab results. But we do know that blood from this wound was later wiped onto one of his paintings elsewhere in the gallery. A painting which had just sold for five hundred and twenty-seven thousand credits, I might add."

Someone whistled through their teeth slowly.

"I know," the chief said. "Bennett wasn't just a

guy on the sidewalk with a doodle pad, like I see some of you are doing instead of paying attention. So here's what we need to figure out: was the whole chain of events pre-planned, right on down to defacing the victim's work with his own blood? Was it a crime of opportunity or passion? Did the killer, during that frenzied moment of violence, see the gash which Bennett received during the scuffle or perhaps due to a fall... and then on impulse also decide to smear that blood, even at the risk of being caught?"

Celia Vickers spoke up. She said, "Has the cause of death been confirmed as strangulation, as opposed to head trauma?"

"Based on eyewitness reports from the officers and paramedics on scene," Paraquez said, "Mr. Bennett's throat was absolutely crushed."

"Then is it possible the wound on our vic's head was actually caused by being struck first?"

"You mean *before* falling? Perhaps with a blunt object? And he was strangled afterward... maybe even while unconscious?"

"Exactly," Celia said. "It's in the realm."

"I'll be damned." Paraquez looked down for a moment, then gave a firm nod. "Now I'm really going to need all of you on point, because our suspect pool just about quadrupled in size. The working theory has been that in order to overpower Mr. Bennett, the killer must have been around a certain age, and—no offense to the muscled ladies of JPC, but the art world attracts a different kind of crowd—we had presumed that the suspect was most likely male."

Some playful boos and jeers went around the room.

"So now, it could be almost any of the dozens of attendees—assuming the theory that Detective

Vickers proposed holds water. And to be clear, there wasn't a comparable object near where Mr. Bennett was found. Our people have already done a full inventory of everything in the room. There's no way they would have overlooked something like that."

"Then we're missing two items," Ash said. "The cloth our killer used to wipe the blood across the painting, and whatever they grabbed to deliver the initial blow. Add that to the list of what tech needs to look for in the footage."

"At least *that* couldn't be flushed away," Paraquez said. "It's got to be hidden somewhere in the gallery still. Unless it was small enough to fit inside a satchel or purse…"

Tessa Helton raised a hand and said, "Do we have any idea how our perp managed to get this guy alone? I'm just saying… big party, busy night with lots of money and action… There's got to be a good reason to step away."

"That's true. Do any of you others twiddling your thumbs have something to offer?"

The team began to brainstorm possibilities.

"Maybe they slipped out to catch a buzz."

"Or to fool around. The cherry on top after making bank selling that painting."

"Could be they were having an argument. Decided to go somewhere private and not make a scene. Tech ought to look for signs of that, too."

"Anything else?" Paraquez said.

"What about a girlfriend or boyfriend?" Tessa asked.

"Hope not," Manny Clark muttered. "I'm getting déjà vu here. Why are all these jilted lovers slicing and dicing their sweethearts?"

"Because homicide's quicker than divorce, smart guy!"

"Alright, settle down," Chief Paraquez said. "I'll

remind you that we're the dogcatcher, not the judge… or social trends analyst."

"Or the marriage counselor," Tessa added.

Manny slapped her on the shoulder and said, "You don't wanna be out of a job, right?"

"How's the private eye business paying these days?"

"You kidding? Cameras everywhere. DNA crawlers everywhere. The damn network knows who's gonna cheat on their one-and-only almost before they do!"

"Not so good then?" Tessa grinned.

Paraquez waited, then said, "To answer the original question, we were able to make contact with a woman named Liz Edmonds. She and Stanley Bennett began dating a year ago, but for the past four months she's been working in Anchorage, Alaska. And according to Miss Edmonds, that distance was not kind to the bonds of their relationship."

"So who was cheating?" Tessa blurted.

"Officer Donnelly, you spoke to her. Fill us in on the rest of the details."

Jay Donnelly stood up and said, "There might have been some of that extracurricular going on, for sure. But she made it sound like this guy Bennett was too caught up in his own work to go see her."

"Hey, love's a two-way street," Manny said. "Supposed to be, at least. Why couldn't she come down here? She a famous artist too?"

"No, she's a scientist. Says she's on contract with some big engineering project up there. Doesn't have time to get away."

"I believe," Chief Paraquez said, "you're referring to the Regal Mountain dig. A huge deposit of minerals was discovered there years ago, and now the machinery exists to access it under the permafrost."

"That's Professor Paraquez to you, folks," Manny Clark announced.

The group laughed, and as the voices died down Tessa Helton mused, "The scientist and the artist. I guess opposites really do attract."

"Until something blows it up," Ash said.

"Detective Buzzkill over here," Donnelly grumbled.

"So? The bodies keep piling up, and I'm seeing way too much of your faces in here lately."

"Feeling's mutual. But what are *we* gonna do, we're just the dogcatchers, right?"

"When the all-seeing eye blinks and the social workers tap out, that's when they call us in. To seal the cracks." Ash shrugged and sat back.

Chief Paraquez said, "Sounds to me like you're all chomping at the bit. So let's see what you've got. The Jacksonville art scene brings a lot of money into town. If you do good, who knows, maybe one of Bennett's colleagues will paint a flattering portrait of the squad."

Manny flexed his arm. "Shirt on or off?"

"As long as you keep your mouth *shut!*" Tessa blasted back.

"What, you don't like these chompers? I floss all the time, for real."

Tessa waved Manny away, but they were both smiling.

"Time to wrap it up," Paraquez said. "I want squad one to digi-scan the gallery for our missing blunt object. Squad two should start analyzing the background info on everyone who attended, especially since the parameters on our suspect have expanded. I want reports on all involved, except for Detective Westgard. We know far too much about her already."

There were a few laughs and exaggerated groans

as the team rose from their chairs.

"And hey, look sharp on this one. *You* brutes may not care, but any artist who can bring in that kind of dough… Let's just say, it's a big deal when they die. Add murder to the mix, and you can be sure a lot of people are going to follow this investigation. So don't get cute while you're poking into these rich folks' lives—otherwise it'll come back to bite us all in the rear. Capeesh? Class dismissed."

Paraquez waved Ash over as the others filed out.

"Walk with me for a moment."

"Sure, Chief."

As they stepped into the hallway, Paraquez continued, "I've got a big problem. That crime scene is a disaster area."

Ash froze. "Did I… screw something up while I was in charge?"

"No, no. The issue is that a hundred people were sticking their grubby hands into every corner of the place for hours and hours. Overlapping fingerprints and DNA on glasses, chairs, the walls, everywhere. Even when we start feeding that data in for the computers to crunch, I don't see how we make sense of it quickly."

"So what do you need from me?"

Paraquez exhaled, then said, "Don't think this means I'm taking the leash off completely, but… I'm gonna need you to dial up one of your Ash specials."

Ash leaned in. "Whose ass do I get to kick?"

"Not so fast, Detective. That may factor in later, but for now just play good cop."

"*Me?* Oh, I don't know…"

Paraquez nudged Ash with her elbow. "You heard me. Because when our vic went down, you were getting to know all of our witnesses as a civilian. Becoming their friend. We've got to capitalize on that personal connection."

"I'm not so sure any of that's left. I pushed 'em around like perps in a lineup." Ash squeezed her hands into fists. "Good or bad, I'm probably just a *cop* in their eyes now. Freakin' disaster!"

"That may be so, and I'm sorry you had a letdown. But right now a murderer is out walking around while we chit-chat. Time to saddle up and commiserate with these witnesses—because while they open up to you, the rest of the team is going to make them uncomfortable as hell digging into their affairs."

"I think I gotcha," Ash said. "Just be a good-enough cop compared to the full-court press our guys are running. Kind of like a social worker, ha."

"Really get to know these folks," Paraquez said more gently. "Listen to what they have to say about themselves. What we need are *insights* into how their minds operate and what motivates them. We're dealing with wealthy and pampered people, not street trash."

"Talented and accomplished, too."

"Exactly. That Muir Gallery has already produced a couple of world-beaters. Meanwhile, JPC... we're local law enforcement, not the FBI. I'm not trying to put us down, but the stakes here are high. That's why I need you on point in your designated role."

"Uh-huh. Screw this up and we all look bad."

"It's gonna be tough. But if we pull this thing off..." Paraquez snapped her fingers. "Champagne and portraits for all."

Ash tilted her head away and tapped her right cheek. "In that case, this is my good side."

"Duly noted. I'll be sure to tell the artist. Now, off you go."

"This dog will hunt. See ya, Chief."

17. A THOUSAND TOMORROWS

Ash went to her workstation and took a deep dive into the life of Stanley Bennett.

By all accounts, he was a rising star in the art world whose obsessive technique was matched by the intensity of his opinions.

"The Obnoxious Philosopher," a lengthy 2044 article profiling his career had called him. Another less-verbose critique came in the form of graffiti sprayed on the sidewalk outside his old studio in Boston. It said, "Shut up and paint!"

And paint Stanley did.

Over the next hour, Ash took in the splendor of dozens of pieces chronicling his development from brash raw talent into a maturing craftsman. As one hastily written obituary concluded, "The world will never know what Stanley Bennett might have become."

Next she watched a short video clip of him speaking at another gallery in Colorado a year ago. While introducing a colleague's latest collection, he said, "The odds have always been against artists. Natural disasters and wars conspire to erase our footprint with walls of water and flame. And yet, in the horrific calm which follows tragedy, we are driven by the creative urge to proclaim that life will survive!

"Artists must always embrace the unique challenges of their place and time. While soulless robotic mimicry is the primary opposing force that we face today, it isn't the only one. People's *indifference* sometimes cuts the deepest, when they don't want to hear or won't look in our direction. I believe the problem is that the once-revered *disciplines* now compete for attention in a society that has become a giant buffet. Fill your plate or sit *on* the plate, the thrills never end—so why even bother trying to elevate the spirit?

"Our century's great famine is of the soul. And yet we're told that artists are the self-absorbed ones… ha! For all our flaws, we are purified by the creative acts which transcend us. The last stand of the individual is being made right now, as proven by every aspirational artist in this showroom who dared to face down a blank canvas in search of the truth. A thousand tomorrows wait expectantly for us to create them. Are you up to the task?"

But there would be no more tomorrows for Stanley Bennett…

Ash suddenly and unexpectedly found herself affected in a way that rarely happened when researching murder victims. She spent her life surrounded by violent death, and understood that personal reactions not only interfered with the work, but had the power to crush you under the weight of all the terror which these people experienced in the final moments of their lives.

So she kept a professional distance. And later,

after hacking through all the lies and veiled clues to capture a killer, maybe the highs felt more like scoring a touchdown than honorably bringing closure to the victim's family. And as for the lows... Ash knew that even if she worked some normal job in the fashion industry, she would always be susceptible to the torrential meltdowns which threatened to derail everything she had built.

The truth was that being a cop gave her good cover. Because in stalking the barbarians which had crashed the gates, homicide detectives did the kind of unpleasant work that no one else wanted to think about while frolicking through this alleged paradise of 2045. So why would *she* ever stop to look in the mirror and risk disgust, when many of the blast craters left in her wake also resulted in murder convictions?

While these criminals ended up caged, executed, or deported, Ash continued to roam free, gaining more and more chaotic momentum with each brazen act that went unpunished, if not downright rewarded.

An icy fear now swept through her, as she sensed that her tenure as a free agent operating with the department's unspoken blessing might be coming to an end. That invitation to the charity gala a week ago had not been extended simply to placate her ego, but also as a tempting glimpse of the good life available to JPC team players. It was a display of how the institution took care of its own, and offered a slice of the pie to those willing to sand down their rougher edges.

Ash had made a genuine effort to clean herself up for that big event, arriving all class in both appearance and demeanor. No wonder she'd caught the eye of preppy Thomas Templeton! Although, she did go that same extra mile for their date on

Saturday night—as if all she ever really needed was a few test spins to get hooked on the square world.

But to go mainstream, you had to be reliable and responsive to the orders that came down from the top. There was no place in this hierarchy for the questionable tactics which defined Ash's brand of policing. Not to mention her off-hours behavior. Her bad habits, her coping mechanisms, her indulgences that obliterated entire weekends…

Something had to give. Deep down, Ash figured she'd likely crash head-first into a wall before ever changing her ways. Because winners always won and won some more… until the day they didn't.

They would have to drag her off the field of life and death, because she would never voluntarily walk away.

And besides, what came after *that*, a desk job?! She'd rather starve. Maybe even while trying her hand at being an artist…

18. CANVAS TIME CAPSULES

Ash had a knack for interacting with the friends, family, and colleagues of murder victims, often tailoring her wardrobe and appearance to ensure they felt at ease in her presence. It was only when cases dragged on, or during dangerous encounters with the criminal element, that she lost control of her adaptive veneer and went ballistic.

But with each new investigation came the renewed hope that she would be able to hold her frame and see it through to the end the right way. The timing and unique circumstances surrounding the Stanley Bennett murder—with Ash on the JPC administration's good side, plus her new crush Thomas Templeton having known the victim—made her yearn even more to solve the crime without reverting to her thermonuclear dark side.

Her first scheduled Monday visit was with Harriet Cohen, a fifty-five-year-old mixed-media artist who had experienced success in previous decades, before settling in as an instructor at a local academy. The woman had attended the auction at Muir Gallery, but left early in the evening and thus was not on the suspect list. Now she wanted to talk to someone from JPC and share her concerns regarding Movement 24.

Ash's fancy dress from Saturday had been swapped for the more sensible outfit of calf-length gray cotton pants, clogs with black leather saddles, and a ruffled blouse in dark rose. Plus a few sprays of sweet-smelling perfume, because seeming approachable often got people talking more readily than when coldly flashing a badge at them.

She also took a car instead of the ATV so as not to mess up her presentation, and thirty minutes later arrived outside the long row of stucco condos which ran four to a structure. She ascended the front steps outside Ms. Cohen's unit and rang the doorbell.

"Detective Westgard, how wonderful of you to come on such short notice."

The woman was slim, with short-cropped pepper gray hair and a deep tan which was in sharp contrast to her pastel linen tank top. Silver-framed glasses, modest gold earrings, pleated navy slacks with brown leather cord belt, and cork flat sandals completed her outfit.

"We appreciate your offer to help. And please, feel free to call me Ash."

"Of course. Do come in."

Harriet led Ash into a wide open living area tastefully arranged with antique-style furniture and many pieces of art on the walls and tables. The room was lit only by the warm midday sun that filtered in through the windows and sliding doors.

"You look familiar," Cohen said. "Have we met before?"

Ash said, "We didn't speak, but I was at the gallery on Saturday night before things went south."

"So *you're* the one who was there. Got it. I happen to know that some of the others are fuming about the police snooping into their lives, but since I left halfway through the bidding and have nothing to hide—"

After waiting a moment for Harriet to continue, Ash prompted, "Yes?"

The woman's face sank. "I am truly saddened by Stanley's death. All I want is to help find out who did it. Because why should *a painter* of all people lose his life like that?"

"I hear you. But in my line of work, it's rarely arch-criminals whose deaths we're called in to investigate. Usually it's the good ones."

"He really was something else, I'll tell you that. I only met him a handful of times, but my goodness, his work! At my advanced age it's all appreciation, however if I was a bit younger, no doubt there would be some envy in there as well."

"Why do you say that?"

"Because," Harriet explained as she pointed a finger skyward, "talent is not equitably distributed, even among the most gifted. Stanley Bennett was on par with *the best of the best*. And now that's all done for."

"I know he was successful, but are you implying that jealousy might be why someone wanted to kill him?"

"First define 'success'. What does that word mean to you?"

"Fame… wealth… parties… sex."

Harriet waved her hand dismissively. "Come on, do better. Much of that can be had by virtually *anyone* these days, easily."

"Then tell me," Ash said, trying to keep her cool. "What am I missing? What is it about you artists that's so different from the rest of us?"

"Look at it this way. Right now the world is as close as it's ever been to an ideal state—and yet we rebel. Countries are at peace, architectural wonders rise up by the thousand—but still we rebel."

Harriet went to the balcony window and brushed the drapes aside.

She said, "Beautiful, isn't it? But I get a bit overwhelmed when I try to take it all in. Instead of peace, I feel an urge to *do* something about it. Whether we're defective ingrates or hyper-sensory freaks, it's difficult for us to just go along with the flow of everyday life. We'd rather turn the mirror back on ourselves and yank out the intestines of our soul for further inspection! I know it sounds agonizing, but that's what we do. Every day. Every night. Searching ceaselessly for the proof that our skeptical instincts were correct. You might even say that we artists are a kind of detective. Yes, I am a forensic examiner of the human condition!"

Ash approached a section of wall where several pieces had been arranged closely together. She said, "Like these? Show me."

"Certainly." Harriet came near and pointed to the most conventional of the pictures. "A lovely portrait painted by a dear friend, who passed away some years ago. Of natural causes, I assure you."

Ash inspected the painting's finer details. In it, a young woman with fair skin looked over her left shoulder while holding a basket of flowers.

"Go to any traditional gallery," Harriet said, "and you'll see many similar works dating back hundreds of years. And yet, those canvas time capsules still speak to us today. Why do you think that is?"

"I really don't know."

"I once spent an entire week asking myself, how could it be? Although I sometimes work in the same medium—in this case oil paints—surely my *intention* is far removed from that of some late-eighteenth-century artist."

Ash motioned to the portrait and said, "If I didn't know that your friend had painted this, there's nothing in the... content or style that would tip me off about when it was done. So is anything actually different?"

"Yes, well..." Harriet blinked several times. "Could it be the relative innocence of the antique painters compared to us worldly post-post-post-moderns? Was this painting here a triumph of my friend's will—or was she no better than some copycatting robot? Perhaps she was saying that the message *has* no message."

"No offense but, who would even think to see it that way? Such a complicated... I just don't follow you."

"A little Art History 101, then. At some point, art shifted away from documentation and expression to... sending an actionable message. This politicization, the urge to always be making some kind of statement, or wanting to change the world... it nearly killed art in the twentieth century. And in our own time, *digitization* of the craft has virtually eradicated the human factor. That's why I say, while this portrait here might not get a second glance from most people, it's always an accomplishment whenever a contemporary artist captures the essence of what it was once all about. *Before.*" Harriet began to sing as she fluttered away, "Before, before, before!"

Ash took a long slow breath. She turned toward the woman and said, "I think I'm starting to get it. But we've strayed pretty far from M-24 and Stanley Bennett. Would you mind if we brought things back in that direction?"

Harriet gave a small exasperated laugh. "What I've just told you took me decades to understand—and an aspiring art student might endure years of frustrating torment to put just *one* authentic vision down on paper. But oh, yes, we must certainly run back to reality and solve this nasty murder. Just remember, some mysteries will *never* be completely solved... which is why I and my kind create." She glanced at the wet bar. "Care for a drink, Ash?"

"Tonic is fine for now, thanks."

Harriet began preparing a cocktail, saying as she poured, "Art really is war, you know. Especially today, when we're fighting on many fronts." She raised a tumbler. "To battle!"

Ash received her glass and clinked. "Cheers."

Harriet then eased back onto a long couch with her feet up. Ash opted to sit across the room on an upholstered chair.

"First and foremost," Harriet said, "you battle yourself, as all artists have done since time immemorial. Fighting your doubts, your demons, your dreams—even against your physical and abstract limitations. But on we march, through disappointment and failure and the thousand micro-deaths required to even *locate* the path which leads to those rare artistic triumphs."

"Success," Ash said quietly.

"Aha! Now you're with me!"

"So all of that even goes into these little pieces here?" Ash motioned to the five glazed figurines that were on the small octagonal table beside her chair.

"Indeed," Harriet said. "Every genuine work is a war won over... entropy, dissipation, doubt. Over anything that tells you *not* to act, *not* to speak, *not* to express yourself."

"And Stanley... Did he win that war, while the

others didn't?"

"That whole crowd over at M-24 has taken the notion of their 'unique proposition' to the extreme. *An* extreme, I should say. Every new school of aesthetic thought must be adamant about doing things their way—it's the distinction that justifies their existence. The danger only appears when these ideas find traction outside the workshop, and the wider world itself wants to have a say."

"I get that money and name recognition can spoil a good thing. But rather than ride Stanley's coattails, someone might resort to murder?"

"Detective, art for us is not just some casual hobby. Or a 'career'. Beyond being a way of life, it becomes *the purpose* of life. So when outsiders start to declare who from your movement is the messiah —especially when he's a non-founding member— that's blasphemy! And sometimes, well, the witch must burn!"

Ash looked down into her glass for a moment. She said, "If Stanley Bennett was outshining everyone else, why not just ask him to leave? Because I'd say it's more than a stretch to think they all conspired to kill him, sorry."

Harriet Cohen scoffed. "I'm not suggesting that! But let me be clear—what we're talking about now isn't at all like Marta Gionet deciding to take her skills in a different direction. No, they couldn't afford to let him spread his divine gospel out in the wider world, if it also meant they ended up forgotten and left to rust."

"Otherwise… what?"

"Imagine working for years building something truly special. A newcomer that you invite to join soon becomes the main attraction. Whenever he decides to leave, maybe the whole castle comes crashing down. And just like that, your empire would be gone!"

"Ah… The brand. Your status."

"The prints and the profits!"

Harriet scooted forward and placed her feet back onto the floor.

She said, "My dear, you must understand that while much of the broader economy is centrally planned, competition remains a very real concept here in the art world. There are definite winners and losers in this cutthroat arena of personal taste. And as a filthy rich man once said, 'Competition is a sin.' "

"A deadly sin, apparently." Ash uncrossed her legs and got up from the chair. "Ms. Cohen, thank you for your time. You've given me a lot to think about."

"My pleasure. I wish you luck… and success!"

19. STREET ARTIST

In the late afternoon—after a workout, wardrobe change back to casual, and vehicle swap—Ash made her way over to the Sprayplex. It was a former industrial area which had at first morphed into a brewery district, before in recent years opening itself up to the underground art scene.

One consequence of the Trifecta's charter to beautify the world was that fringe forms of expression such as graffiti were often squeezed out of the public square. But Jacksonville, like many metropolitan areas, had been successfully petitioned to allocate space for "the unrefined arts," so that unconventional as well as underprivileged creators might also practice their craft freely.

"God bless the steam valve," Ash said to herself as she rumbled her ATV through streets lined with bright murals that overwhelmed the senses. Even the traffic signs, light poles, and electrical boxes were decorated in colorful patterns.

She pulled into a small parking lot in back of a

whiskey tasting room. A slim but muscular man wearing a paint-spattered t-shirt and baggy orange cargo pants was up on a step ladder, applying blue accents in careful spurts. He looked over his shoulder when the engine cut out.

Ash took off her helmet. "Are you Devon?"

"The one and only. You trying to get that bike repainted?"

Ash dismounted and glanced at the airbrushed smoke finish on her ATV's armor plates. "What's wrong with this?"

The man stepped down and shrugged. "Nothing, I guess. But I could do better."

"Yeah well, I'm not in the market for any… art investments right now."

"Hey, just trying to drum up some business. 'Cause these spaces are *not* cheap!"

"No problem. How long's your… lease?"

"Got it for three months total. I'm about two weeks in, hope to be done with this piece here end of next week. Then it's time to collect! Photo-ops, merch, you name it. Now lemme guess, you're here for the interview, right?"

"Not *that* kind of interview." Ash chuckled and showed Devon her badge. "But don't freak out, I'm just here with some questions about Stanley Bennett."

"Oh," he said quietly. "Well… Detective Ashley Westgard, I heard the news and it hurts like hell. But I'm on a tight schedule, so the work can't wait. Maybe I'll paint a little something for Stan later on."

"I'm truly sorry for your loss. And rest assured, *my* work is completely focused on finding out what happened Saturday night. So anything you can offer might help me crack the case."

"How should I know? I wasn't there." Devon frowned. "But alright, if you say so. Ask away."

"For starters," Ash said, "I heard you two were close."

"Yeah? Who told you that?"

"Does it matter? Come on, help me out. I'm trying to solve this thing. What can you tell me?"

"He and I go back, for sure. But as you can see, we ended up on… different corners." Devon waved a hand at the surrounding buildings, where a few other artists were also at work. "Guess he liked being inside. Safer than the streets—or not."

"How long ago was that, uh, fork in the road?"

"It's been a minute. I mean, we got together some after we found out we were both here in Jax. But not lately, 'cause really, it's better to be with people that's already on your same page."

"Or wall." Ash cracked a smile and tilted her head in the direction of Devon's mural.

"Yeah, yeah!" he said. "Exactly. We all wanna be unique… but still, it helps when you don't always have to explain yourself."

"Got it. So tell me this—how much do you know about Movement 24? Did you spend any time with them?"

Devon scraped the toe of his shoe against the pavement. "That crew's weird. I don't really hang out with those guys unless it's a networking type of situation. Too much peacocking for my taste."

"How so? In their art, how they act, or… ?"

"Okay, look around you. What we do out here is *street* art. Big and bold. Loud colors, crazy shapes —a shock to the system! Because the life we came up in was rough, always *in your face*. No quiet, no rest, and sure as hell no chance to learn how to paint like they do in the big galleries. But! We got just as much spirit. Maybe more, 'cause we had to fight so hard. Did whatever it took to get our hands on a can that was almost tapped dry, just so we could say

with those last few drops, 'Hey, I'm still here.' So…
now you know."

Ash looked over Devon's in-progress design—
when completed, it would cover the entirety of a
wall that was twenty-five feet high and fifteen feet
wide. The misshapen letters and jarring facial
expressions took on a deeper meaning than her first
impression, which had been instinctively negative.

She saw a cluster of disheveled people huddled
near the bottom. They were being trampled by
someone much larger whose face lacked any readily
identifiable characteristics. Above the fray was a
shirtless man very much resembling the artist
himself, except that the eyes and physique had both
been exaggerated to extreme proportions.

Ash turned back toward Devon and said, "You
battled to survive. But sometimes… even when you
get away, it doesn't always go away. Right?"

"Could be."

"Same for Stanley as well? Rough start?"

"I'd say so. Bunch of us all found each other at
school. 'Unmotivated students,' they called us. Truth
is, you can get a hell of a lot done in life when no
one cares either way."

"Is it possible he kept some of that attitude or
hard edge, even after reinventing himself as a
mainstream artist?"

Devon picked up a new can and shook it
aggressively. A loud clicking sound broke the silence.

He said, "From what I remember, it was a big
relief when he got out. Like, he was gonna try and
forget the whole first part, not 'tell his story through
art' or whatever. Didn't want to be people's little
rescue pet, reliving the ugly over and over just
because the customers had money."

"I see. So—"

"Hold up. I need you to be clear on one thing.

Stan maybe went legit at the beginning, but that group he got mixed up with is like a cult. I don't care who the patrons are or what museums they're in, that's how I feel."

Ash kicked at a bit of trash that was on the ground and said, "I don't see much in the way of robots around *your* workspace, Devon."

"Like I said, *a cult.* There's plenty of ways to live your life how you want, and not have to talk about what you *don't* like all the time."

Ash watched Devon scoot an extension ladder along the wall, climb up ten feet, and spray orange streaks across a dark circle.

She said, "Alright... bear with me. You've covered a lot and I want to get it straight. First, what do you think was really going on inside M-24? Because I spent some time at their space, and they all seemed about as strange as any other sort of artist I've met."

Devon sighed and climbed down, coming close as he said, "Look, I understand you're doing this investigation, and I want to help you find out who killed my friend. But I'm still in this scene, too— and you just never know who's listening that might be holding the gate key. This location here, I had to wait on a list for eight months just for the interview! So now, it's time for *me* to cash in and get mine."

"Christ... I hear you." Ash walked in a small circle, then said, "I can't stop you from looking out for your own interests. But if M-24 is actually dangerous, I need to know what's going on before maybe someone else gets killed."

"I've told you what I think. Honestly, I don't much care for most so-called artists anyway. A kid using crayons is sometimes more legit. And maybe the peacock does his dance 'cause he likes people blowin' smoke up his behind. If that's art, I say let 'em have it."

"However you may feel, the clock's ticking for me. I can't afford to waste time running down dead ends. So, last chance if you want to help me get your friend justice."

"Oh, now you're gonna pull out that card? Goddamn…"

Devon tossed his spray can onto a rumpled drop cloth and shook his head.

After a silent moment, he said, "If you really knew what some of us went through back in the day, and how much evil some people got away with… Point is, *I* made it through. Give me space to do these paintings, let me work it out. I ain't Stan, so hell yeah I'm gonna tell the world what happened!"

Devon stared up at his mural. The fading sun had just disappeared behind another building, and now the vivid scene looked flat and dull.

Ash felt herself struggling to keep the conversation going. At last she said, "I see dead bodies all the time. I've got dried tears in my clothes from the mothers, husbands, and kids of these innocent victims. So it's fine if you want to challenge the whole world to a fight, I get it. But you don't have to fight me."

"Stan was a good dude. He wasn't… *bad*. Everything else is just whatever." Devon waved a hand at the wall. "Maybe it's right that these all get covered up with something else. Be crazy to put stuff this heavy in a permanent collection. It's too much for people to handle."

Ash watched him sling a jean jacket over his shoulder and walk slowly toward the whiskey bar's rear entrance. He didn't turn back to offer her a drink inside.

The interview was over.

20. ENVY

"Oh, hullo there, Ash."

Thomas Templeton's face appeared on her dining room wall. He was standing outside of a building and shaded from the morning sun by several large palm fronds.

"Hi, Tommy!"

She was unable to contain a bashful smile, despite not having heard from him since he left the gallery early on Sunday.

"So how is the investigation coming along?"

"We're trying. It's just a lot to get through with so many possible witnesses."

"I'm sure you'll do fine." Thomas gave a quick salute.

Ash took a step toward the camera. She said, "But… I do have tonight off. Was thinkin' maybe we could get together?"

"Ah… about that. Afraid I won't be able to swing it."

"You sure are a hard man to pin down."

"Well, while you've been out searching for clues, I decided to do a little hunting of my own."

"Into the case?" Ash said, perking up with interest.

"Bah!" Thomas waved a hand carelessly. "I wouldn't dare step on your toes. But since I haven't been allowed to pick up my auction prize—it being locked away inside your crime scene—I turned my attention to another item on my list of must-haves."

"And?"

"A remarkable four-panel sequence called *Lost Seasons* has just come up for sale. The astronomical asking price means I'd be a fool not to do a visual inspection before buying. I'm at the hangar now preparing for my flight."

"Oh," Ash said quietly. "But hey, you're not leaving the *country*, are you?"

"Erm, well…" Thomas offered a guilty smile. "I already gave your people the slip on my way here. Think you can cover for me?"

"Thomas! Where are you going? No—don't tell me. But… when will you be back?"

"A quick jaunt, I promise you. And upon my return, we'll have an evening out. Perhaps a cruise on the waterway, just the two of us?"

"You own a boat, too?!" Ash said with exasperated excitement as she smacked her forehead. Subconsciously, she was also a bit annoyed at herself for letting Thomas get her hopes up, knowing that he might find an excuse to cancel later.

"Not here in Florida," he said. "But I do have ready access to a few vessels around town. For now, I must bid you farewell as I embark by air."

"Well, alright then. Hope you have fun on your trip."

Thomas laughed. "I always do! Don't work too hard while I'm gone."

Ash raised a hand, but he had already signed off before she could wave goodbye. She felt her spirits, her heart, her everything just *sink.*

"Damn."

Glancing around the apartment at nothing in particular, Ash suddenly saw everything she owned as being terribly inferior. While not cheap or haphazardly arranged, none of it was good enough for a man of Thomas Templeton's stature. And so the life which Ash had made for herself... now it didn't really seem all that great.

Here was the risk of looking in on another world where the grass was demonstrably greener—you might never be satisfied with your own lot again. But Ash was no penniless orphan! She was a high-flying, heavily armed detective doing real work for the citizens of Jacksonville. So why this dreadful feeling of envy?

Because Thomas had flipped the script on her, as if he represented something unattainable that Ash wanted secretly and desperately—when for as long as she could remember, *she* had been the prize.

The absurdity of it all was driving her insane! She didn't have *time* to waste on wishy-washy suitors. Not when there were vicious criminals to add to her rogue's gallery of captures. Wild adventures waiting to be had with her girls. And new conquests to write into the legend of her own gloriously sordid biography.

The Life and Times of Detective Ashley Westgard.

The *finest* among Jacksonville's finest. Lover. Fighter. Loner. A hurtling meteor impervious to both damage and doubt. Until now.

Who was this aloof Thomas Templeton to exploit her blind spot and take advantage of that rare flaw in her constitution? How dare he force her to crash-land in this foreign realm that was lush with thoughts of a future where one cooperated, rather than ravenously consumed?

Yes, that was it...

Beyond her fantasy image of that life of leisure on Caribbean beaches... Beyond plotting to outwit, defeat, and psychologically *crush* Thomas before tossing his bones along the side of the road... Lay the prospect of harmonious partnership without the fear of betrayal, and deep sustaining contentment instead of being a hostage to endless cravings.

It was the ultimate terror.

To sit in perfect stillness. To not be plagued by the need to always do, take possession, or turn the spotlight onto herself. To be rooted in a sense of belonging, rather than feeling compelled to lace up the boots each day on that insatiable quest for validation... justification... and impact.

Now it all seemed possible—but at what cost? If your whole existence had been spent frivolously or in error, what would be left of *you* after stepping onto the other path? And would some destructive inner voice linger to try and coax you back with promises of even greater mountain peaks?

Ash brought a hand up to her heart. She needed to parachute away from this stratosphere of imagined joys, because right now Thomas Templeton was boarding a private jet and might never call her again.

If she succumbed to this hopeful reverie and later found herself left in the lurch, she would almost certainly triple down on her worst instincts —and hell knew no fury like that of a deputized goddess scorned.

Without thinking, Ash went into the kitchen and snatched the blue mum Thomas had given her from the windowsill. She threw it down the sink and ground it to bits in the disposal.

"I'm very sorry, sir. We seem to have lost your luggage."

She laughed, but the rest of the apartment remained quiet and empty.

21. TOO MANY ANTENNAS

Ash was instructed to meet with Muir Gallery director Roger Vance on Tuesday afternoon. He greeted her at the front entrance and led her to a small wing which had been closed to the public on auction night.

"If you'll please just excuse me for a few minutes, Detective, but I absolutely *must* finish the call I'm on. Have a look around and I'll be with you shortly."

Vance disappeared from the large doorway.

Ash stepped further into the showroom. The air was cool and her shoes tapped audibly against the polished wood flooring. All was silent throughout the gallery—the JPC's forensic team had completed its meticulous digital survey of the property, and now only two robot sentries kept watch outside.

The first piece that caught her eye was the sculpture of a nude female. Carved out of marble, or possibly some synthetic material, its faint lavender hue shimmered under the angled ceiling lights. The facial expression was flat, with dead eyes staring out into nothingness—but Ash still sensed a profound beauty in that stoic pose. What had this woman witnessed and then refused to turn away from? Or was she perhaps being subjected to leers and ridicule, yet stood resolute in the face of such harassment?

The left arm lacked most of its wrist, and the delicate hand was connected by way of a square-sided metal bar.

"I see you, M-24," Ash said quietly.

She next approached a wall where each piece had been hung so that the viewer could absorb it without interference from the others.

One painting featured a geometric theme, and its four-foot square canvas was filled with a dizzying array of intersecting colorful shapes. Ash noted that here too, one jagged area the size of a plum had been left blank in the painting's middle-left.

Moving on, she beheld a mixed-media work entitled *Artifactually Incorrect*. Slightly larger than the previous piece, this was a collage of children's playthings which had been affixed to the navy blue canvas. Once again, a triangular portion of the top left corner was bare.

Ash had just glanced at the Virgin Mary painting, when she heard footsteps enter the room and the director say, "See anything that strikes your fancy?"

She turned away from the enormous canvas, noticing at the last moment that the eyes of Baby Jesus had not been rendered.

"These are interesting," she said slowly. "Not sure I appreciate all that's going on with them, though."

The man smiled broadly. "Ah, but that's the point. Great art should be savored over the course of a lifetime. We can't expect to fully comprehend a piece after only a single viewing. Shall we?"

Ash followed Roger Vance through the main gallery into the back hallway, but when he entered his office she paused and said, "I want to see the crime scene again, actually. Do you mind?"

"As you wish," he said politely, and led Ash back to the end of the corridor. He hesitated. "I have your formal permission to enter?"

Ash nodded and he waved a tiny key fob in front of the latch, then pushed the door open and tapped absently at a sensor that activated the ceiling lights.

The twenty-by-twenty space had white walls and an unfinished concrete floor that was dotted by paint droplets here and there. On the left, easels and stools were arranged in a semicircle around a square dais that sat in the center of the room. Ample evidence of police and paramedic activity remained on the right side, which also housed two large cabinets and a handful of supply carts.

"Was this room locked on Saturday night as well?" Ash said.

"Yes," Vance replied. "It wasn't needed at the time, so keeping the door shut was easier than making it presentable for the public."

"Then… how exactly was the body found again?"

"I believe that the guests wrangled someone with a key to open the door during the mad rush when everyone was looking for Stanley—and then they came upon the gruesome scene."

"Who else besides you has access?"

"Well, let me see… All of the artists, of course. Plus the members of my staff… Various donors and patrons… Oh, and some special 'friends of the gallery,' as well. It's a nice little perk for hobbyists to access the private studios from time to time."

"That sounds like a lot."

"What can I say? There's a lot of trust in this family."

Ash glanced around the room. "What's this normally used for?"

"Most recently, group figure study. Sometimes it's good for everyone to come together and sketch the same subject. They then discuss the state of each artist's personal style."

"Who models for that? Does one of them get drafted... or?"

"Not at all, ma'am. At this high level everyone must stay in their own lane. There's certainly no lack of eager volunteers to sit and take off their clothes. Because, to be able to call oneself *a model*... who wouldn't bare it all in front of a group of strangers, when *these* strangers happen to be artists?! Ah, what a funny world we live in."

Ash glanced at the dais. Any other time, she might very well have savored the opportunity to step out of a silk robe and wow a group of sketchers with her own goddess-given, weight-room-crafted work of living art. But the fact of the matter was, three days into this case and all she wanted was to be done with it as quickly as possible.

She refocused and said, "Mr. Vance, tell me about the role of a gallery director when it comes to being the... representative or public face of an art colony."

"Order out of chaos," the man said with a snap of his fingers. "That's the best way I can put it. Even in setups like M-24, where a group has coalesced around a philosophy rather than simply because they're all friends, you still need a captain or guiding hand."

"To keep them all rowing in the same direction, you mean?"

"That, and to help them stay out of trouble."

"Hmm. What sort of trouble?"

Roger lowered his voice. "Detective, the artistic personality has always been seen as somewhat unstable. And while yes, later on the world gets to enjoy the fruits of their labor, far too many of them are downright insufferable—brilliant or not! I serve as a buffer between them and the general public, for the benefit of all."

"Kind of like a team manager the night before a big game?"

"*Someone's* got to keep them focused on amplifying this school's message. Because I'll have you know, exciting new fads pop up all the time and lure people away."

"You sound skeptical, and yet this is your profession. You *profit* off their work, but also think of it as... a whim?"

The director took a deep breath. He said, "Please, don't take my candor to mean I'm dubious or exploiting anyone. Let me explain. Any artist will tell you that they have an endless supply of ideas—and *I* think the reason their lives are so exhausting, is because they were born with too many antennas attached to their heads! I see this struggle all the time, and I truly sympathize. Their minds are never *quiet*, but also seemingly incapable of looking far enough ahead to *plan*. So here I humbly stand. In the thankless role of steward, school principal, or heaven forbid... father figure."

Ash allowed the man a moment as he carefully unfolded a kerchief and dabbed at his temples. She said, "I'm grateful for the explanation. I wasn't trying to put you personally on the spot."

"No offense taken. We've all been out of sorts since this tragedy happened."

Ash nodded, then said, "How good are you at

sensing when a group is about to fall apart?"

"Well," Vance replied, "calling myself the captain isn't just a metaphor. As the head of a gallery, I've got to know when to turn the rudder… or even abandon ship."

"Right, right. So tell me, did you notice any warning signs over the past few weeks?"

The man sighed. "I've seen it all in my day, Detective Westgard. The feuds, the intoxication, the sexual dalliances… Their volatile lives are a cautionary tale!"

Vance threw out his arm and whacked one of the easel frames. It rocked around on its three legs before coming to a standstill without toppling over.

Ash pursed her lips and said, "What were the red flags?"

"It wasn't the usual indicators that I normally look out for. Half the time, ideological differences aren't even what split these movements up. No, it's the classic human foibles: jealousy about fame or lovers, or one member getting credit for a new technique that ten of them probably developed together over time. No, Stanley Bennett was fixated on the idea that everyone should excel. He didn't want M-24 to rest on its laurels and risk losing relevance, so he kept pushing them all."

"And how did they respond?"

"*You've* seen what's on display in my gallery. The answer should be obvious."

"So no tension at all?" Ash said impatiently.

Roger Vance shuddered. "There have been some squabbles, yes. But that's not uncommon, and these petty disagreements often pass without incident."

"What does your gut tell you—would anyone from M-24 actually have it in them to kill Stanley?"

"I should hope not! And why are you singling *them* out? What if it was a disgruntled bidder or some crazy fan who did it? Have you even considered those possibilities?"

"We're looking into everyone who attended the auction, sir. But if it *was* an inside job, what might have been the reason?"

"I don't know! I suppose… If I could go back in time and give Stanley any type of warning, I'd say to ease off. Let everyone enjoy their time in the sun. Because M-24 has plenty of momentum."

"I see." Ash folded her arms and looked down. "At the end of the day, it really is all about doing business, huh?"

"I'll admit that," Vance said. "But please understand, most artists who make it big already come from money. It should be no surprise if, underneath their berets, you also find a silver spoon."

"But not Stan. He grew up poor."

"Very much so. Clawed his way to the top on merit and ambition alone. I'm afraid he never fully internalized how his scrappiness, which was so admirable early on, might later strike people as being too overbearing."

"The obnoxious philosopher, right?"

Roger Vance clasped his hands, then said slowly, "He just couldn't accept that in the world of monetized art, despite all the high drama during the auctions, nothing is ever truly urgent. And setting the spiritual component aside, we must also admit that art is never actually a matter of life and death."

"Nope." Ash glanced at the roped-off section of the room where Stanley Bennett had taken his last breath, then tapped her holstered pistol. "Not until it bleeds over into my department."

22. GREATNESS AND TRAGEDY

By Wednesday, the investigation was congealing to a standstill. All of the technical data had been collated, examined, reshuffled, and appraised again. The sparse event footage was pieced together for simultaneous playback and analysis. The hundred attendees were all being looked at from new angles.

But there had been no major breaks in the case. Any promising leads had proven inconclusive, witnesses were unreliable or not forthcoming, and the killer hadn't made a false move yet.

Ash was staring at her work computer screen, fists clenched and desperate to make some sort of connection, when her intercom buzzed.

"Detective Westgard?"

It was Chief Paraquez. Ash felt a surge of dread —maybe the clock had run out on the JPC's chance to solve this important case.

"Yes, boss?" she said. "What's up?"

"Head down to interrogation. We've got a fresh fish."

"Yeah?" Ash nearly jumped out of her chair. "What's the word?"

"One of our attendees was caught trying to break into Muir just before dawn. The bots on watch grabbed him. A Professor Giles Nelson. Ring a bell?"

"Uh… I must have read the name, but I don't think I met him."

Paraquez paused. "Okay, I'm sending you his info. We've let him sweat for a couple hours. Now I want you to pick him apart."

"With pleasure. Thanks, Chief."

Ash gathered some materials relevant to the case and put them in a nylon attache, then went to the restroom to freshen up. She gave herself a hard look in the mirror.

"Let's do it. Gut 'em and fry 'em."

She was buzzed into a gray interrogation room a few minutes later. Entering slowly with an intimidating swagger, she only turned to face the man after reaching the table where he sat.

He was small and pale, with tight wrinkles and reddish freckles on his face. Not the type of physique likely to overpower the younger and more robust Stanley Bennett in a fair fight—but then again, homicidal rage *was* a source of strength known to beat the Vegas odds.

The man looked up expectantly while Ash unpacked her tablet and files.

She said, "I didn't realize that art historians also moonlighted as cat burglars. What do you have to say for yourself, Professor?"

"It's not what you think," Nelson pleaded and buried his head in his hands.

"Please feel free to explain. I'm inclined to say you went back to the gallery to retrieve the murder weapon."

Nelson looked up, his face contorting in pained confusion. "Murder wea… ? Oh, no, no, no. You think I *killed* him?"

Ash nodded. "We know you were there on Saturday. Right now my team is pulling up every fingerprint you left and tracing every step you took. My guess is that soon, we'll have a pretty good idea of how you convinced Stanley Bennett to leave the party so you could whack him."

Professor Nelson sat stunned. He licked his lips, then said quietly, "My only crime was attempting to preserve his legacy for all time. I never laid a hand on him, I swear it."

"Then explain your behavior this morning. Because a quick glance at your file shows a mousy little bookworm who never so much as stole a bagel, let alone committed any violent crimes. So if you don't have a guilty conscience, what would drive you to risk throwing it all away now?"

"His painting… *The Tower*. I needed to get it out of there."

"You greedy bastard! Were you planning to sell it and live large from here on out?"

"No!" Nelson shouted. "I love art, I *live* for it! These past few days, all I could think about was how some slimy opportunist would find a way to extort the world with Stanley's last painting. I couldn't bear the thought of it and I lost my head. I went to *rescue* it, to ensure that all people would have the chance to behold this final testament to his greatness."

Ash watched the man wilt back into his seat. Carefully she said, "Let's say I believe you. That this was a well-intentioned act of reckless loyalty. Why you? What do you bring to the table that would justify handing the painting over to you?"

"Because *I* get it. *I* have the eyes that artists wish

were universal. I'm the one they paint for! Which means I'm also the translator helping the average person to understand art more clearly."

Ash decided to dial back the pressure. Now that the man was talking, she felt he would either confess to the murder in his own time, or had in fact only been foolish enough to try and break into the gallery.

She said, "Giles, I'm here to listen. We don't want to convict the wrong guy for killing Stan. So lay it out for me."

"Thank you." Professor Nelson took a deep breath. "It's like this. Everyone thinks that everyone else is either at their own intellectual level or *below*. Only a genius can conceive of the possibility that another person might actually be smarter than them —just as it takes someone perceptive to realize that we don't all see the world through the same lens."

"It takes a genius to recognize genius, as they say? Which makes you what?"

"Never mind me, and that line is too clever for its own good anyhow. Much too simplistic. I believe that if you are earnest… and humble… and adore the *idea* of the hero, then you don't have to be one yourself in order to foster the process."

"Like being a part of the network, that kind of thing? Critics and agents and reviewers?"

"Yes, but… the implications are more substantial. This goes beyond sales, beyond publicity and awards. Some people just *know*. They instantly grasp when an artist has synthesized all that came before—and then taken the next step forward."

"Lemme guess. Stanley Bennett's work was on that level?"

"You're not getting it! What was exceptional beyond his own exceptionalness, was that his genius had actually been recognized in the moment. How many musicians created a new sound that could have propelled their sub-genre forward, but there was simply no one capable of understanding the significance at the time? Or maybe the infrastructure wasn't in place to promote them far and wide? The worst scenario is when nobody has the courage to enter the kingdom, even after being presented with the key."

"Come on," Ash grumbled, "people want to see movie magic. They like music with big production."

Nelson's face turned red as he said, "But only when that kind of entertainment makes the audience feel good about themselves! Real geniuses use art to lay down the law, which causes us to stop and say, 'What is *this?* So it's not really all about me? Maybe there's something more... and also wonderful?' " The man went limp and said flatly, "Which is why I think we live in hell."

Ash gave a shrug. "It's one beautiful hell, then. Food and clothing for all under the twinkling lights of skyscrapers."

"Oh, forget the robots and the material things. Think about how *culture* might evolve if people transcended their own egos. Not simply to find God, either, but to help uplift the geniuses who live for nothing more than to bestow their gifts upon us. We would experience an endless cascade of great leaps forward, instead of waxing nostalgic about generational victories like the Trifecta or the invention of the microchip."

"Look," Ash said, "I took a deep dive into Stanley's career. I saw his paintings. They're really good, don't get me wrong. But I think it's a stretch to compare his work to the scientists who figured out how to get a robot to repair itself. So what am I missing?"

"That most *people* are also robots in spirit. They're too scared to stand out from the crowd. Too needy, too entitled, on and on. *Real* robots engage with the conditions they encounter and then adapt— while we self-sabotage and will probably lose out in the end. Sadly, there won't be any honorable passing of the torch on that fateful day when we collapse into the dustbin of history. I wonder if the machines will even bother to pick it up afterward."

Ash shook her head doubtfully. "I don't know about all that. Countries everywhere are thriving because of what the Trifecta started. There's more First World than Third World now—and you *don't* have to be a genius to see it!"

Nelson closed his eyes and said wearily, "I just know that something crucial has been lost, even if *you* don't believe me. It's the end of magic and mystery, because the system is so afraid of unpredictability and the possibility of suffering. As if dark times weren't what forged our species, and often brought out the best in us."

"There's still the mystery of who killed Stanley Bennett. Which I, an actual person and not a robot, am trying to solve."

"No disrespect, but police business is strictly a *reactionary* affair. By mystery, I mean how we have all been dropped onto this confounding plane of existence, and that those of us who dare to look upward await the moment of revelation. Otherwise…"

"Otherwise, what?"

"It's all been a cruel joke. A tormenting illusion where the rare artistic feats, which we believed were glimpses into a world of better possibilities, turn out to be a reach too far. And thus we are mere prisoners, stranded alone in this godforsaken kingdom of confusion and pain."

Ash said, "Maybe you can afford to hide away when the going gets rough. Not me. I've got to stick around and plug these bullet holes, before the world drowns in an ocean of blood."

Professor Nelson reached his hands out humbly. He said, "I do believe we're both on the same side. Working for good. I deeply apologize for my little dalliance earlier today, which has caused you all so much trouble. A criminal genius, I am not."

Ash stood up to leave.

"They may want to hold you overnight. I'll try and put in a good word for you on my way out."

"And the media, will they be told? My god, if this gets out it could ruin my career…"

"I don't know what to do about that yet. I mean, if we hold a press conference and say there's a suspect in custody, maybe the real killer will get sloppy. Hey now! That was a really great idea. Thanks, Professor!"

As Ash turned away with a mischievous smile, she saw Giles Nelson fall forward onto the table with a wailing sob.

"Jesus, man! I was only kidding…"

23. ALL THINGS EARNED

She tried to focus on the task at hand. A full workout crammed into half an hour in her own living room. It had been done many times before— just enough sets and reps of each exercise as part of a scientifically proven regimen that ensured maximum efficiency and results.

But for all the precise moves and encouraging affirmations she recited aloud, this routine couldn't prevent Ash's thoughts from leaping back to the case. And so, instead of controlling her breathing and watching her form, she kept picturing Stanley Bennett down on the floor beside her—and dying in the prime of life.

She set aside the dumbbell she had been using for tricep kickbacks, then dabbed at her forehead with a towel while quickly appraising herself in the mirror. Looking good, but careful fine-tuning was required to maintain that perfect balance between muscle tone and lithe femininity.

A man like Stanley Bennett would scoff at this

fitness obsession, or the two-hour process she went through while getting ready for a special event. *He* could just grab a ratty wool jacket and show up as-is, because what he arrived bearing was so much more powerful than any *effect* that Ash the blond bombshell could hope to achieve.

Bennett was *natural*. Born with the molten fire of the universe sloshing around his soul, he had spent the entirety of his life in the mad grueling effort to throw a saddle over top this formless energy and channel it into something great—and far greater than himself.

The proof was out there for all to see. His body may have been zipped into a bag and stuck inside a freezer down at the morgue, but his vitality continued to radiate from a hundred art connoisseurs' collections.

Ash cast a quick dismissive glance at the seductive wall calendar that the JPC's press department put out—its September page featured a tantalizing picture of her wearing a blue bikini. But to equate pushpins with picture frames was an insult to all things *earned*. Or… manifested.

On the day of her photo shoot last year, Ash had simply shown up at the beachfront location and spent several hours as a pampered passenger. Wardrobe options were provided. Her hair and makeup were fretted over by professional stylists. And some lanky female photographer from Austria had made sure that Ash looked her absolute best over the course of a thousand shutter clicks.

However many dozens or hundreds of those "Beach Babes on the Beat" calendars existed, eventually they would all come down off the walls, with most being recycled or otherwise destroyed. A small fraction might be saved by her personal admirers, but Ash figured she would find those guys creepy if she ever actually met them in real life. Still, she couldn't help but wonder if maybe her friend Vernon had acquired one as a memento after their brief fling a while back…

Being selected as part of the calendar's roster had been a big deal for her at the time, but was now losing its luster like a piece of fabric that spent too much time out in the sun. Ash Westgard knew she just wasn't in the same league as Stanley Bennett, even though *he* was dead.

She dropped onto the floor mat and began a set of fifty cross-body crunches.

Why was she even comparing herself to him? Or… how dare she compare him to herself? *She* was the nobody. Born beautiful and at age twenty-seven already locked into a stable career with the police department, Ash was well aware that her smooth path didn't hold a candle to the inexorable rise of that poor boy from Illinois.

He had fought against fate and won, by reaching a much higher pedestal than anyone imagined possible. But Ash had landed pretty much where most people would have expected—for now, at least. She wanted to believe that she also possessed some of that boldness, even if she didn't yet have the vision or discipline to use it for more than chasing after thrills…

She kicked her legs out and flipped over into plank position. As she held the pose and her stomach muscles tightened, a bead of sweat trickled down her forehead to the tip of her nose, until she exhaled with her lower lip jutting out and sent the droplet flying away.

While the herd puttered along in boring oblivion, Stanley Bennett's chaotic tornado of a mind had blazed an indelible path across every canvas his brush touched down upon. Although he may have died long before exhausting the supply of ideas stored in his spiritual vault, there was no denying that his brief existence had been a success.

Surely his sense of creative satisfaction on the evening of his death was far greater than the thousand-and-one forgotten momentary triumphs that comprised the nocturnal biography of one Ashley Westgard...

A terrible realization buckled her at the knees: only blind ignorance and the full bank account of youth had enabled her to live a complete inversion without ever suffering the consequences.

Then, just as despair over her irredeemable failings threatened to freeze her soul solid and cast it down into glacial waters forever... she suddenly saw with choking clarity the distilled essence of all that Stanley Bennett had embodied.

No disguises. No hesitation. No excuses. The world be damned, he had always done the work.

Ash pushed up to a standing position and squared off against herself in the mirror, gritting her teeth as she sent a jab at the reflection of her face. Defeat was not an option. Right now a murderer was out there breathing the fresh free air, while the talented hands of Stanley Bennett would never hold a paintbrush again.

She *had* to find his killer! To prove that she was just as good at her craft as he had been at his own. Because for all her faults, all the self-destructive wastefulness of her private life, whenever Ash rocked that JPC badge in pursuit of society's worst offenders... never was she more pure in motivation and deed.

She turned away from the mirror and headed for the shower. Her workout was done, and soon it would be time to resume the hunt...

24. BEYOND ART

Everyone seemed to be accounted for. Everyone was eager to vouch for the whereabouts of their colleagues and friends. They were all appropriately shocked and crestfallen. They had all been having far too much fun to notice that anything was amiss. Wine, good vibes, and money had been flowing freely. People were on the lookout for *more*, not danger.

The few available pictures and videos of Stanley Bennett had proved ambiguous. One moment he was happy and mellow, the next animated and getting into it with someone. But trying to read anything into that came from a skewed perspective: Bennett didn't know he was soon to die, and others in attendance could also be seen venting frustration or anger at times during the night. The real truth about what happened to him might not be found within the sparse piecemeal footage currently in the possession of the Jacksonville Police Corps.

Even the security video acquired from the

surrounding buildings had come up empty—anyone who left the gallery before Ash locked it down had been cleared of suspicion. She and the rest of the investigation team were stuck in a rut.

Ash, who had so often utilized the surveillance grid's blanket coverage of the city to review fateful moments and identify suspects, now began to wonder if cops *and* computers might always miss something during technical analysis of the data. Actions could be read into too deeply, or motivations not revealed by words alone. This paradox seemed destined to remain an unbridgeable gap, as more lives were extinguished in flashes of violence that shocked both perpetrator and victim.

And if artists were already engaged in a perpetual struggle to express what it meant to be human, how could a local cop like Ash expect to account for the vilest extremes of criminal behavior?

Simply put, she was stumped and getting frustrated.

After everything she had learned about Stanley Bennett and the local art scene, she still couldn't reasonably surmise why the killer struck the way they had. There were fifty possibilities bouncing around her head, with each leaping from the plausible to the ludicrous and back again.

At last, Ash had to accept that she needed advice from someone outside the case—but it came at the cost of swallowing her pride.

She made her way down the main hallway on the third floor of JPC headquarters, peeling off into a winding artery and then leaning silently against a doorframe with her arms folded. She waited.

Nearly a full minute later, the man who was seated inside the small office finally glanced up from his dual-monitor workstation.

"Oh," he said with a grumble. "It's you."

"Howdy, Ted. What's the word?"

"Still working for a living. Someone's got to put two and two together."

Ash motioned to the empty swivel chair in front of the desk. "May I?"

"By all means. To what do I owe the honor?"

As she sat down, Ash watched him deliberately slide the nameplate emblazoned with *Detective Theodore Gillard* up to the desk's very front edge. It was a not-so-subtle reminder to keep her boots on the carpet.

"Got a riddle for ya," she said in the most ingratiating tone of voice she could muster.

Ash had never treated Ted well during their pairings together on cases in the past. This included shutting him out of the dramatic late-night raid which led to her invitation to that gala where she met Thomas Templeton. (Still no word from *him* in two days...) She resented having to ask Ted for help now, knowing that it was her own immature behavior which justified his coolness toward her.

"I'm trying to figure out a motive."

Gillard nodded slowly. "I assume this is about what went down at Muir Gallery? A close call for you, eh?"

"Something like that. So you already know about the case?"

"Anyone with an ounce of culture would have heard about the Bennett killing. And understood what it meant."

Ash raised a hand defensively. She opened her mouth, ready to lash out—but instead offered a smile. She couldn't afford to alienate Ted right now, and if she took the bait about him claiming to be so sophisticated, which also implied her own lack thereof... They would just end up rehashing the many pointlessly tense conversations had while out on the job.

It was Ted the one-legged anachronism versus Ash the headstrong climber. Not much of a team within the larger paradigm of AI-powered systems bleeding over into their niche of police work, which so often relied on gut instinct to connect the dots. But truth be told, they *had* solved their share of crimes together...

She said, "And that's why I'm here. With uncultured hat in hand. Because we've already done a ton of grinding on this thing. Got all the raw data, did interviews, pieced together what little of the footage there was. Even drew up a decent personality profile on this guy Bennett. But clearly, we're missing something."

Ted leaned forward. He said, "What's got you chasing your own tail? Too many possibles or not enough actionable leads?"

"It's not even that. I can't figure out why it was done then and there. That seems to be the key to everything."

"Okay, shoot."

"Let's say I have a grudge against the victim. He copied my style, stole my girl, is getting too big for his britches, whatever. The point is, I could kill him in any number of places without taking the risk of being caught in the act there at the gallery."

"I follow," Ted said. "Whack him back at his studio, or on a nature hike. Although, there are cameras, cameras everywhere... and often in places we wouldn't expect. Sometimes being in a big crowd can actually help obscure what you're doing."

"Ah, goddamn, that's right!" Ash snapped her fingers angrily. "Which totally screws up one of my theories. Because now... Christ! Did the killer know that the security cameras would be off all night? If *that* was the reason for the timing, then killing Bennett at the gallery wasn't symbolic at all. It was strategic!"

"Slow down, Ash. If you have another hunch, don't toss it away just yet. Let me hear what else you got."

Ash sighed. "Okay, my original idea was that for someone to kill Bennett publicly, on everybody's big night, maybe it was meant to send a message to someone else."

"Who? A potential next victim?"

"I don't know! Did some agent screw the killer over in favor of Stan, and he just had the bad luck of becoming collateral damage? Or did he *represent* something our killer despised, and they snuffed him out in a manner that would make everyone take notice?"

"Now you're cookin'," Ted said. He took hold of a walking stick, and his titanium prosthetic lower leg creaked underneath his slacks as he slowly stood up. "This sounds big, no matter how we slice it. Assuming one thing, that is."

"And what's that?" Ash said tensely.

"Are you truly *convinced* that the murder didn't happen in a moment of absolute madness?"

"I want to believe it was planned. Gill, they smeared Bennett's blood across his own painting, for Christ's sake! That is a textbook psycho stalker-type move."

"Ash, I know all about it. But just picture this." Ted leaned his weight onto the side of the desk. "Bennett and I are chatting after the auction. He's feeling good because he made a sale. Something sets me off, I grab the nearest heavy object, and wham! Suddenly that torrent of rage, which every person has the capacity to unleash in the right circumstances… it opens up all the way after I deliver the first blow, and I don't stop! Do you follow? Bennett is dead in a matter of seconds, and this person who five minutes ago was perfectly calm, now literally has blood on their hands. The situation has gone beyond logic—beyond art, even! He or she has tapped into the primal animal living back in the wilds of prehistoric nature. So in that irrational haze, why *wouldn't* they march right up to Bennett's painting and announce their victory? Who knows, maybe the odds were good that no one else would notice—because while they were all in party mode, the killer alone had entered this other realm of existence."

Ash watched Ted thump his chest, then dropped her own head into her hands.

"Oh, man," she groaned.

"What's the matter? Am I way off base?"

"No, you're not off, and that's the problem." She looked up at him. "I might be back to square one. I was almost certain this was all premeditated, but now thanks to you, impulse has to go back up on the board. Ted, what the hell am I supposed to do?"

Gillard jabbed his cane forward. "You gotta look at that footage again with new eyes."

"But there's barely anything to work with! It's mostly still shots, and all the videos are being jerked around at eye level. It's a mess!"

"Doesn't matter. All you need to focus on is body language. Facial expressions. Because even if the killer *did* plan it a week or a month in advance, there's *no way* they could completely mask their emotions in the immediate aftermath. You know it, Ash. Only the most cold-blooded sociopaths can pull off that kind of an acting job. And they're a rare breed, thank God."

"You're right," Ash said with a small sense of

relief. "And if there's one thing I've learned about this crowd, they're *real*. Wearing their hearts on their sleeve, and telling you *exactly* how they feel."

Ted laughed and eased back behind the desk.

He said, "Go over all the visuals again and you'll see. *Someone* is on top of the world. And not because they won an auction or sold a painting, either. Find the face that's overflowing with satisfaction… and triumphant arrogance."

"Do you think," Ash nearly croaked, "they might be emboldened enough to do it again?"

"Could be! But find out the *who* first. After that, you can try getting into their head."

"Thanks, Ted," Ash said as she rose to leave. "You never miss a beat."

"Mind over machine," he mused. "Because I too prefer the animal within. As for the rest, what can I do?" He tapped the cane against his metallic ankle.

"Later, Gill."

"Go get 'em, Detective."

25. THE ENGINE ROOM

"Stop it there, Val. Go back ten seconds and slow it down."

Ash was leaning forward on both hands, darting her eyes between the three giant screens which displayed all available views inside Muir Gallery on Saturday night. Each camera had been allocated its own rectangular quadrant, and these spaces flickered on and off as still photographs and short video clips played in sync with the official timeline. One of the tech squad's best operators was at the controls running it all like a sophisticated ballet.

"Rolling 'er back," the woman said. The frayed cuffs of her denim overalls dragged along the Berber carpet as she scooted her swivel chair back and forth. "And here we go."

As the footage played at half speed, Ash zeroed in on several looks at the gallery lobby. There was so much going on here that she had already reviewed the twenty-minute window of primary interest five times. Now she was tightening the dragnet, although she couldn't pinpoint what specifically triggered her mind a moment ago.

While she *had* begun by targeting that look of exhilaration which Ted Gillard believed would be the giveaway, Ash soon discovered that nearly everyone was caught up in some form of delirium after the auctions ended. There was the drunken clinking of champagne glasses. Smooches on the cheek and surreptitious whispers. Dramatic poses struck in front of just-acquired art pieces. Small groups dancing along with the music that was playing in the background. And even some views of Ash herself...

Now she was forced to refine her search like a virologist increasing magnification on a sample slide. She scrutinized the subtlest nuances of body language for a nervous twitch, a clenched fist, or rapid blinking... *anything* that might stand out from the general mood of celebration. The night had been young, and everyone ready for action...

"Should I keep looping this part or play more?" Val asked.

"Damn, I don't know... Wait! What the hell is that? Nudge it back and hit pause."

Seconds later, Ash pointed at one of the frozen images.

"Zoom in on her. What's she doing there?"

In the frame, behind the three people who were smiling for the camera, a squatting woman could be seen fiddling with one of the larger sculptures.

"Play it forward, real slow."

Val steadily tapped a button to advance one frame at a time, while Ash's eyes moved quickly from screen to screen.

"There she is again! Go back one."

The same woman was now visible in a video clip that panned from left to right across the gallery floor. Her expression was serene, with eyelids half closed and her back arched as she floated out of view.

"No… freaking… way." Ash started to sweat. "She looks like she's in *the zone*."

"Ma'am?" the tech said.

"Okay, okay… Maybe she was just stoned. Uh… Tell the system to isolate her from every vantage point. I want to see where she goes and where she's been. By the way, what's our timestamp here?"

"We are t-minus three minutes until things go sideways."

"Okay, lemme think. Can we see the Bennett painting anywhere right now?"

Val manipulated her controls for a moment and *The Tower* came into view.

"Whoa," Ash said. "That seems stained to me. Which would mean everything's already happened. We gotta go back! No, wait. First let's play it through until the chaos actually starts. I want to see our girl's reaction."

The system had completed Val's request to track the woman of interest, and now a reddish halo appeared around her while she stood leaning against the bar. During the several minutes that elapsed between someone first calling attention to Bennett's canvas and the subsequent discovery of his body, the woman continued to sip her drink calmly.

"Man, she sure is savoring that cocktail," Val said. "Not a care in the world. What are you thinking about, lady?"

Ash couldn't resist a smile, despite the magnitude of what was happening on screen. "C'mon Val, don't tell me you wanna be a detective too?"

"Nah! Wind beneath your guys' wings is enough for me," the tech said as she popped a piece of gum into her mouth and spun around in her chair.

"Good. 'Cause you're doing great right now."

"So… is that your killer?"

"Maybe? Probably… I hope so."

"Sick. So whaddaya need me to do next?"

Ash steadied herself. "We have to trace her steps one at a time. See how—see *if* she even did it. Like I said, maybe she was just totally wasted and had no clue what was going on."

Val cued the footage back three minutes to when they first saw the woman kneeling in front of the sculpture, then slowly played everything in reverse. Flickers of red materialized here and there whenever the suspect came into view.

The woman first walked backwards into the hallway where the studios and lavatories were located, before showing up in the gallery once again.

"You're gonna do it, aren't ya?" Ash said as she watched intently.

Other people were dancing in a conga line… the woman was also twirling nearby… one moment Stanley Bennett's canvas was stained red… and when it next came into view, the top right corner was stark white.

"God… damn. I am gonna run this town one day!"

Ash pointed skyward as she strutted around the darkened room.

"What's this all mean?" Val asked.

Ash leaned in beside her and said, "It's playing backwards, right? So in real life, first she uses something to wipe the blood on there, then a minute later she flushes it down. See ya, evidence!"

"Ohhh, crap."

"Good luck trying to find it, too. Probably been turned into a pair of socks by now. Machines one, M-24 zero, baby!"

While Ash laughed, Val groaned.

"I… kinda… wish you guys gave me more material to work with. Don't get me wrong, I catch a lot of bad dudes and dudettes in here, but this one's tough. We really haven't *seen* anything yet."

"Yeah, but…" Ash felt her head swoon. She knew what had to be done next, roughly speaking, but still the swiftness of this potential breakthrough had nearly given her a panic attack. She took a breath and said, "Everything's fine, Val. You work the keys and I'll work the angles."

"You got it, Westy!" The tech cracked her knuckles and began jotting notes onto a pad. "So this is the one who did it, huh? Know her name?"

"Samantha Minn. She designed that sculpture we just saw."

"So… an artist-on-artist murder? That's pretty epic! How do you think she killed our vic?"

Ash said, "He was strangled, but maybe got knocked out cold first. And if I remember right… oh, man… there were a bunch of birds mounted inside that walnut."

"You think she broke one off and went after him with it?"

"It's possible. But let's both be smart and see if the footage shows anything else. Who knows, maybe it really was the part of the sculpture she left incomplete. Which would mean… M-24 with the comeback win, alright!"

"Why do you figure she did it?"

Ash wagged her finger at Val. "Now, now, Dee-*tech*-tive. You and I still have serious work to do. We need to map out everything that happened, step by step and clear as day, so that people can follow the chain of events. And hell, I better get Chief P. in here. She's gonna want to watch it go down in real-time. Otherwise *I'll* get nailed for aiming too high."

"Everybody's got a boss," Val said as she bobbed her head happily. "But *I* rule the engine room."

She typed a sequence of commands and the video montage resumed.

26. A DANGEROUS GAME

Chief Paraquez took her place at the front of the briefing room. Every crease and seam of her navy blue polyester uniform was immaculate. At forty-three, she was still a sight to behold. Smooth skin naturally toned. Piercing black eyes. A five-foot-four rocket from Miami built in perfect proportions.

But no one dared to let their gaze linger for too long. The chief was a scrapper at heart, and the years of administrative duty had only increased her powers, like a martial artist who could defeat adversaries with words alone.

Standing next to her in sharp contrast was a buffoonish man of sixty. A red polka-dot tie and matching kerchief were the standout features of his otherwise bland look—slate gray suit, brown caterpillar mustache, and pale drooping jowls.

"Okay, everyone," Paraquez said, "I'd like you to meet the newest member of our task force. His name is Kyle Holmes, and some of you may recognize him from the accounting department. But today he's playing the role of Curtis Walther, a wealthy art collector from Madison, Wisconsin. Sir, we welcome you!"

The man gave a salute and bowed his head. He said, "Thank you, Chief, for putting your trust in me. I won't let the team down."

"Now," she continued, "here's the deal. As you've all been briefed, our person of interest is Samantha Minn. The evidence against her is more than circumstantial, but we're still awaiting fresh lab results to determine whether she used some part of her sculpture to assault Stanley Bennett. More importantly, we can't afford to spook her. Because as we've all seen firsthand, this art clique has the money, the means, and the *attitude* to protect their own. One tip-off that she's under suspicion, and we might never see Ms. Minn on this continent again."

The chief rubbed her fingertips together.

"So instead, we're going to indulge her vanity. Let her know that in the wake of her colleague's death, and the mad scramble to acquire his works which has already begun, she too is still in high demand. Our collector friend Mr. Walther has been in touch to express interest. A rendezvous at her loft has been arranged for later this afternoon. And *we* will be there as well. Any questions?"

"How's an accountant gonna get someone to admit to murder?" Manny Clark called out.

"Thank you for your concern, Officer Clark," Paraquez said. "But the purpose of this exercise is to put our suspect at ease. Our decoy only needs to keep Ms. Minn occupied briefly while we move in to make the grab."

"She might hit *him* on the head, too," Tessa Helton warned. "Good luck, buddy!"

The group began to chatter loudly and Paraquez raised her arms to cut them off.

"I know, I know. We're aware of the risk, and Kyle has been advised to keep his distance. But remember, we believe that Ms. Minn caught Stanley Bennett by surprise. Now it's *we* who have the upper hand in that regard. Any other concerns?"

Jay Donnelly held up a small tablet. He said, "I've just been reading the transcript from this lady's interview, the one she gave at the gallery right after the killing."

"Yes, and?"

"At one point she says, 'Art can be a dangerous game. Some people push the boundaries too far, and then society pushes back.' What do we think this means, now that she's our main suspect?"

Chief Paraquez consulted her notes. "It looks like... Okay, I see. Officer Leonelli took that interview, but she only filled in on Saturday night and hasn't worked the case since. Detective Westgard, you've been a sort of co-pilot with me on this. Please step up and give the team your perspective."

Ash had prepared for this moment. A chance to demonstrate leadership qualities when so much was on the line. To prove that her management of the crime scene hadn't been a fluke, and she really could do more than twist arms for answers out in the streets. She had gone over Samantha Minn's interview twice, and also put on a respectable pantsuit for the briefing. Besides, there was already a set of raid-appropriate clothing waiting inside her locker for later...

She rose and stepped forward, placing her own materials on the podium as Paraquez stepped aside.

"Thank you, Chief," she said. "Our suspect is thirty-four years old. Born in London, but her family moved to San Francisco when she was a child. As an artist, she's had residencies in Chicago,

Philadelphia, and Montreal. The recent rise of Jacksonville's art scene brought her here eighteen months ago. Other than that, Ms. Minn has no criminal history, no episodes of domestic violence, and no political activity to speak of."

Paraquez said, "Officer Donnelly just asked about that odd statement she made during her interview. What's your take?"

"Right." Ash motioned in Jay's direction. "I watched the whole thing earlier. First, in the context of the event—a wild night of celebration turning into a murder scene, and with all these big personalities involved—I'd have to say there's nothing particularly alarming about her statement. But in light of what we think we now know, her suspicious if not downright incriminating actions before Stanley Bennett's body was discovered..."

Ash trailed off, wondering how best to convey the intangible aspects of what she had learned about the case.

She said, "Okay, it's like this. The type of art we're dealing with here involves more than the works themselves. It also goes beyond money, which may be hard for us working stiffs to understand. None of them are ever actually *starving*, but if you sell a painting for fifty thousand, while someone across the room rakes in four times as much... That affects the ego, no matter how enlightened you profess to be. Why? Because you put your *soul* into that thing! How can it be worth a fraction of someone else's?"

"Why not kill the bidders then?" Jay Donnelly said. "You can't blame other artists for what's popular. I just don't believe that one disappointing sale would drive a professional artist to murder. They'd probably just paint something new!"

"Good call," Chief Paraquez said. "But what if

your numbers fall short consistently?"

"If I may," Ash said, "I was told by my acquaintance Thomas Templeton that Ms. Minn's sculptures have been doing very well. In fact, the giant walnut you've all seen sold for over two hundred and fifty thousand credits."

"And now it's booked into evidence," Manny Clark said with a laugh. "Wonder what it'll be worth after the trial?"

"Never mind that," Paraquez said. "Let's focus on motive, people. Samantha Minn alluded to artists living in danger, as if they were always courting disaster. What did Stanley Bennett do to provoke *her* into killing him?"

"Allegedly," Celia Vickers muttered under her breath.

"It wasn't the money," Ash said. "We've also found nothing to suggest they'd been romantically involved, so jealousy doesn't seem to fit the bill. What else?"

"Maybe she's just crazy," Tessa Helton said. "Too much booze or drugs, then he did something that made her lose it."

"But going to the trouble of removing a bird from the sculpture, then leading him away from the party with it hidden in her bag? No, in a moment of true rage she'd just let him have it."

"Allegedly!" Celia said more loudly. "There's barely any visual proof of them near each other in the lobby. And nothing at all from the back hallway."

"That's true," Ash admitted. "But I feel like after the… *alleged* murder, we've got enough probable cause to take some sort of action."

"You're absolutely right," Chief Paraquez said, first nodding at Ash before staring down Detective Vickers. "Which is why we're doing it this way.

That Samantha Minn might be one cool customer. To nonchalantly defile Bennett's painting, and then not show any remorse during the interview afterward… We all need to look sharp today."

"Be careful in there, guy," Tessa said as she pointed to Walther the decoy. "She might see right through your act. Then it'll be lights out! And all of us here would be personally devastated if our paychecks got delayed next week."

"Alright now." Paraquez rapped a knuckle against the lectern to quiet the jeers. "Mr. Holmes is in fact a minor art collector, so he knows his stuff. We'll have surveillance in place all around the property where Samantha Minn lives, plus he'll be wearing a body cam. Now, that's enough talk. Let's suit up and roll out—it's time to catch ourselves a killer!"

27. GETTING UGLY

Ash rode to Samantha Minn's building in the back of an unmarked van along with five other members of the task force. In total, twenty people and three auxiliary bots would participate in the operation, with Chief of Detectives Gabriela Paraquez in command.

But when the vehicles parked in an alley nearby, Ash and the others were informed that Samantha Minn had been spotted by the surveillance squad leaving home fifteen minutes prior. As Mr. Walther's meeting time approached with no sign of her returning, Chief Paraquez began to pace nervously.

Finally she said to the decoy, "You, Holmes. Head over there and ring the bell like normal. Hang around for a few minutes, then try to call her."

"Will do," the man said, then shuffled off in his clownish outfit.

The team crowded around a small screen which a tech had set up. Kyle Holmes soon arrived outside the large converted warehouse which Samantha Minn shared with other working craftspeople.

Ash stepped close to Paraquez and said quietly, "I don't like the feel of this. Something isn't right."

"Maybe so," the chief said. "But I was assured by surveillance that Ms. Minn didn't dash off in a hurry. She wasn't carrying travel bags or anything like that."

"Hmm. So *we* haven't tipped her off to make a run for it. But something has her spooked. Otherwise, why would she risk blowing a sale?"

"I see what you're saying. Sam's a pro like the rest of them. A businesswoman in a paint-splattered sweatshirt."

"Whaddaya say… take a look around inside?"

"Who?" Paraquez said. "Send in a bot scout… or you?"

Ash gave a friendly smirk. "You know how much I feed off this kind of action."

"Okay, but…" Paraquez motioned to another female officer in tactical gear who was standing nearby. "Hey, Green. C'mere."

The woman with light chestnut hair tucked a necklace inside her shirt and approached. "Ma'am?"

"You and Detective Westgard are going to pop in for a little sneak peek. Follow her lead. I'll alert the rest of the squad that you're moving in."

A minute later, Ash was trotting down the alley with Officer Green at her side. For now her pistol remained holstered under her left arm and concealed by her vest—but ready for a quick draw if necessary. They swung around behind the building, then looked for the best way to enter.

"There," Green said. "That big swinging door isn't shut all the way."

"Good call," Ash said. "Your first name?"

"Jo."

"Alright, Jo. I'm Ash. Let's move, nice and quiet."

They shuffled forward and slipped through silently, then Ash secured the door once they were inside. This back area was a chaotic jumble of canvas frames, large trash items, industrial supplies, and charging stations for the janitorial bots.

Ash glanced down at her bracelet screen and brought up the building's floor plan.

"Down this hall," she whispered, "then left. Unit 12."

"Got it," Jo replied. "Lead the way. I'll cover you."

Ash began a breathless sprint through the warehouse's long corridors. She paused at a split, peeked her head around the corner, then lurched forward with Jo Green less than ten feet behind.

They came to a tall, gray metal door. Ash crouched low and pointed at the lock.

"Can you open that without leaving a scratch?"

"No prob." Jo reached into a cargo pocket and produced a black rectangular device. She held it near the hardware, and a few seconds later there was an audible click. "Knock, knock."

Ash took the curved silver handle into her hand, rising as she pressed down and slid the door open. She darted her head inside for a quick glance, then removed her pistol and entered the space cautiously.

All was still. Natural light came in through the curved skylights thirty feet above. Feeling her heart pound with excitement, Ash began a silent and methodical survey of the loft while Jo mirrored her movements on the opposite side.

The front living room arrangement had four couches and a giant square coffee table where Ash saw mugs, wine stems, and a snack plate. The fancy kitchen off to the right was dark, but a wine bottle and cork on the counter were visible.

Moving deeper inside, they reached a structure in the back left which had been framed and walled off from the main area. A dresser and a bed lay beyond the open door. Jo Green, her compact rifle raised, slipped through like a ghost.

Ash angled further right into a wide open space that ended at one of the building's corner walls. Several windows higher up provided additional light for what was evidently the workshop. It was a cluttered maze of raw materials, in-progress works, miscellaneous tools, and several completed sculptures whose style was instantly recognizable as being Samantha Minn's.

She was just about to turn back toward the front of the loft to explore the metal staircase she'd seen on the far side of the kitchen, when a ray of sunlight reflected off something on the floor. Something wet.

She raced over and looked down. It was blood. Drops... leading to a small pool... then smears... running all the way to a closed door at the back of the same buildout which Jo had entered elsewhere.

With her gun pulled up against her chest and all senses hyper-alert, Ash slowly eased along the wall toward the door. She put her free hand into her vest pocket and used it to turn the knob. The room was dark, but she quickly spotted a sink and a toilet. As the door swung fully open and bumped against the right side wall, daylight poured in to reveal more blood on the floor.

She entered nimble as a cat, and stepped carefully to avoid slipping or disturbing the mess. She approached the shower, then slid the curtain back with the barrel of her pistol...

Ash felt herself exhale heavily.

Stuffed into the tub was the portly body of a

middle-aged man wearing a dark business suit. Although the light was dim this far into the room, she could see the matted hair and dark stains on his badly damaged face.

Something blocked out the sun behind her and she whipped around toward the door.

Officer Green was standing at the threshold in silhouette, with feet apart and her weapon at the ready. It was an impressive sight, and Ash was relieved to have Jo watching her back.

She said, "Call the chief. The meeting with our decoy is canceled."

"Oh yeah?" Jo said as she shifted her weight. "What you got?"

"Another body." Ash tucked her pistol back into its holster. "Another guy I met on Saturday night."

"This is getting ugly."

"You're telling me…"

28. MIX AND MATCH

"Find out where the hell she went and get back to me."

A tense Chief Paraquez ended her call and waved at Ash. They were standing in the far back corner of the loft near Samantha Minn's workshop, with the fateful doorway in view. The task force had moved in quickly and set up a perimeter around the warehouse, and those inside were now awaiting the arrival of forensics to begin analyzing the crime scene.

"Yeah, boss?" Ash said.

"The surveillance guys are scrambling as we speak. Minn leaving like that took everybody by surprise. I suppose they expected her to come right back in time for the appointment—but goddamn!"

Ash had rarely seen the chief so flustered in nearly two years of working under her command. She waited a moment and then said, "Looks like somebody else had a meeting with her first. Our friend from accounting is lucky to be alive."

Paraquez folded her arms. "That's what gets me. We've had eyes on the building for hours, and they didn't see our victim enter. So if he's been here most of the day… why'd Samantha suddenly decide to kill him?"

"I don't know how closely you looked around, but there's a bunch of food and drink stuff up front. I think he and Samantha were having a little party."

"I did see that empty wine bottle, yes. Seems like everyone was having a good time before Ms. Minn snapped. Now tell me about our corpse—you say he was at the gallery on Saturday?"

"Yeah. Dimitri Something. A real social butterfly making the rounds. Seemed to know almost everybody. Always going in for hugs, smooching cheeks, that sort of thing."

"And did you personally meet him? *Before* Stanley Bennett died, that is?"

Ash thought back to the moment when the short and stout Dimitri had looked up at Thomas, his black beard curving into a delighted smile as he said, "And here is the handsome Mr. Templeton! How are you, my friend? And who is your stunning companion?"

This was followed by nearly five minutes of polite banter, as Thomas and Dimitri went back and forth reminiscing about past gatherings and the artists they admired. Although Ash couldn't keep up with their conversation, she smiled agreeably whenever she was on the receiving end of Dimitri's glowing compliments.

"But the time has come, that I must leave you in the hands of this charming lady," the man had told Thomas before virtually skipping away toward another festive group.

Now addressing Chief Paraquez, Ash said, "I remember. He's a critic. Big time, from what

Thomas told me. Lives up in Nashville, but apparently did a lot to help the Jacksonville art scene break out."

Paraquez nodded in the direction of the bathroom where Dimitri's body lay. "Not a very nice way for Sam to repay someone who helped *her* pay for all this square footage."

"What the hell set her off?"

"Do you think he knew... or suspected? Could he have come here to blackmail Samantha, and maybe arrange to take a cut of all her future sales?"

Ash glanced at one of the in-progress molds that sat on a wooden crate. She said, "I find that hard to believe. The guy seemed really genuine behind all that hot air. He was like a kid in a candy store. All those people, the big event... it was his *joy!* I can't see how he'd be willing to soil himself, or it, with any dirty dealings."

"If you say so," Paraquez said dryly. "But that means we've got nothing. I'll have to call tech and tell 'em to analyze that footage yet again, this time with Dimitri in the spotlight."

"Before you do that, come take a look at this."

Ash led the chief over to one of the workbenches. It was littered with sketches, scraps of raw material, paint tubes, and a variety of brushes and tools. She reached into a cardboard box and removed an unpainted hawk. First she rapped her knuckles against the rock-solid cast body, then pointed to the underside. Protruding out behind two small leg holes was a thick rounded nub with horizontal grooves that resembled a light bulb cap.

Next she pulled a model branch from a tall wicker basket that was loaded with an assortment in different lengths, textures, and thicknesses. She indicated a recession in the surface of the branch, then began to screw the hawk into place. Halfway through the process she stopped and twisted it free, before taking a second bird from the box and securing that in the same socket.

"See? This way, Samantha can mix and match while working on her designs."

Paraquez nodded. "But does she permanently glue them in place, once she's decided which bird goes where?"

Ash said, "Let's find out."

They went over to the nearest completed piece, which was an open-faced acorn the size of a car tire. Ash reached inside the diorama and gently grasped one of the four vibrant cardinals that sat perched on brown branches. It swiveled smoothly, and the flexible little legs adapted easily to their new position on the branch surface.

"Of course. You can make them face whatever direction you want."

"Ohhh," Chief Paraquez said. "So she didn't use the… incomplete or broken part of her walnut to attack Mr. Bennett. She actually had *options*."

Ash stepped away from the sculpture.

She said, "Imagine getting clocked on the side of the head with one of these chunky birds."

"A solid blow could knock anybody out. Plus the sharp beaks… tails… and that bump on the bottom. No wonder he had a gash."

"Yep. Brutal. And I'll bet that working with all this bulky material has made Samantha very strong."

Paraquez glanced around the workspace. "Now what about this guy Dimitri… were you able to locate the bird, or whatever she used on him?"

"No, ma'am," Ash said. "I got wrapped up trying to figure this out while you and the team were racing over here. The place is too big anyway. I have no idea where she might've hidden it."

"It'll turn up—it's either here or she took it with her when she skipped out."

"To what, toss off a bridge?"

"No matter what she tries, there's sure to be cameras on the route. So if Sam's out digging a hole somewhere, we'll track the thing down eventually."

The chief brought a hand up to her ear and closed her eyes.

"Hold on… Uh-huh. Yeah. Okay, got it." She looked at Ash. "We have a new location. Time to move."

Ash gave the bloody floor a final glance, then followed Chief Paraquez toward the exit. The chase was on.

29. LOOKING UNDER ROCKS

The van was tense with anticipation, now that their *suspect* had been confirmed as a killer.

The task force's next destination was a complex of ritzy condominiums across town, where they would rendezvous with the reinforcements Chief Paraquez had requested.

Ash was pressed close against Jo Green along the left side wall of the van's darkened interior. Officers Manny Clark and Tessa Helton sat across from them, each looking down at something on the screen of his wristband.

"Nice going back there, Jo." Ash raised a fist and they bumped tactical gloves. "You moved just right. I hate when shadows step on my heels."

Green nodded. "All good. It's a team sport. Sometimes you get the ball, sometimes you block. The goal's the goal. And that's it."

"Right. So… I don't know how all this is gonna play out, but I want to catch our girl alive. It's time to get some answers."

"About why she did it?" Jo looked directly at Ash for a moment. "I mean, why do we do anything sometimes?"

Ash grumbled. "No, that's too easy of an out. I wanna know why she threw her whole life away for… what, exactly? To shut up a couple of jerks? 'Cause all that money, all that fame… it's not gonna save her now."

"True."

"It's funny. When I was there at the gallery, I totally got sucked in by the… what do you call it… the spectacle, I guess."

"You think it was all BS?"

"Eh… more like being hypnotized. Or not listening to your gut. Yeah, that's it. You start to think that all we do at JPC… maybe it's not important. And in fact, we're wasting our time going out looking under rocks for trouble. So nah, I don't need them—*or* him. This is the real deal right here."

Ash thumped her elbow back against the side of the van.

"You found the trouble, alright," Jo said. "And here *we* are, chasing her down like any other nobody."

"That Samantha sure did it up in style. Doesn't make her any less of a murderer though."

"What it means," Jo huffed, "is that someone'll probably make a movie about her life one day."

"Christ," Ash muttered. "And we're part of it. *We* are gonna be in that damn movie. *Painted* in whatever light they feel like." She paused for a moment, then said, "One more reason we really need to make a clean capture. If our names are gonna be plastered on TV, I don't want it to be because we were the ones who shot Samantha Minn."

"You hear that, y'all?" Jo said loudly. "No one goes trophy hunting today. We bag this bitch alive!"

As the others grunted in response, Tessa and Manny giggled and poked at each other while watching whatever was playing on his screen.

"Hey," Ash said. "You two a thing now?"

Tessa smiled and looked away.

"Maybe," Manny said, slitting his eyes as he glanced from Ash to Jo. "And what about you?"

"No comment." Ash adjusted herself on the bench. "Plenty of work to do before the sun goes down anyway. So stay focused."

"One step at a time, boys and girls," Tessa said in a soothing voice. "For now, teamwork."

"That's right!" Manny shouted. "It's all about the Corps…"

The three nondescript JPC vehicles arrived at the Palm View Gardens property fifteen minutes later, then pulled around back to park outside the delivery entrance. Each team took a service elevator to the ninth floor, then separated to the corner stairs and climbed up an additional level.

"All units, hold your positions."

Ash received this message in her earpiece, as did every other member of the raiding party. She cleared her throat and leaned back against the stairwell wall.

"Now we wait," she whispered.

She used the downtime to check the laces on her boots, as well as the safety on her weapon.

"The unit number is ten-nineteen," the broadcasting voice announced. "Schematics are being sent to you now. The front door is centered, with a living room on the left, dining area and kitchen to the right. Two bedrooms are in back, straight ahead. Please hold."

Ash glanced down at the screen on her wrist as the condo's three-dimensional floor plan appeared. She held her arm out in front of Jo Green, saying quietly, "Big balcony next to the living room. Gotta make sure she doesn't jump."

"I dunno, blood and bone on concrete could make for a real work of art."

"Damn, you're cold. How have we never met before?"

Jo shrugged. "Just saying. You know they'd turn it into a shrine afterward. Tourist destination with posters and t-shirts for sale. I can see it now."

Ash clenched her jaw, tapping her toe anxiously as she said, "Come on, come on. Let's get in there and make the grab already."

"Countdown," the dispatcher said. "Prepare to move in sixty. Reporting two inside. One female, one male. Teams A and C, exit your positions and converge outside the target location. B team, move to the nearest adjacent corner and wait for further instructions. Go!"

Ash gave Jo's shoulder a punch. "Rock and roll."

"Come to Mama…"

Their team of four shot down the carpeted hallway with silent speed. They paused at a turn, then hugged the left wall while making the final approach.

A second group was moving toward them from the opposite side of the building—six imposing figures armored in black, their pockets bulging with tactical accessories, and carrying both lethal and nonlethal weapons.

"Wait," the voice instructed. "Steady now… engage in ten, nine, eight…"

Two members of this other squad stood up and

lugged a long heavy object forward. In silence, they slowly rocked it back and forth, then slammed the blunt end against the right edge of the door. The fifth deafening hit broke it open and everyone began to pour in, entering alternately from the left and right sides. The breach team dropped their battering ram and followed closely behind.

Ash was third inside the unit. She hunched low and moved to her left, pistol raised and shouting into the din of howling voices.

"Police... police!"

"JPC! Don't run!"

"Hands... let's see 'em!"

Two figures stumbled out from one of the bedrooms, their faces both stricken with terror.

Ash saw Samantha Minn try to shield herself from the many grabbing hands. And...

A man... very tall... eyes wide as he staggered forward.

Thomas.

She felt herself swoon for an agonizing instant. All the years of police training and mastering the rules of the street had prepared her for firefights, gory crime scenes, human misery, anything...

Almost anything.

She tried to snap out of her daze by falling in with the swarm, but was suddenly stricken by a crushing double doubt.

What was *he* doing *here?*

"C'mere, you!" she heard Jo Green shriek while seizing Samantha Minn by the hair.

Ash's mind locked firmly back into war mode.

"Split 'em up!" she yelled. "Sit her down, and put him over there. Dammit... we gotta check the rest of this place. Move!"

Ash motioned toward the bedrooms, then she and three other team members ran inside to ensure that no one else was present. Advance intel from dispatch was valued but never ironclad, and so it was essential to also secure locations visually.

"Clear!" a voice hollered from the room next door.

"Clear in here!" she echoed, then took a giant heaving breath. Her head was throbbing, and she had to wait a moment for the rush to subside before stepping back into the main room.

Samantha Minn, flanked by two intimidating officers, sat helplessly on a floral love seat.

Ash approached with restrained fury. She said, "Oh, Sam. You naughty, naughty girl."

"*Me?* How could you possibly… ?"

"Just shut your mouth. We know." As Ash began to walk away, she glanced over her shoulder and added, "Bird's the word."

The sculptor's face went white, and she covered her mouth as it began to tremble.

30. WATERCOLOR

Ash stared plaintive daggers at Thomas Templeton. He gave her a sheepish look from his stool at the raised breakfast bar. She waited until the shackled Samantha Minn was escorted past them out the front door before speaking.

"I really don't know where to begin," she said. "Are you... a suspect... potential victim... accomplice... or what?"

Templeton, whose hands were zip-tied in front of him, gave a shrug. He said, "I am completely innocent in this matter. Although I might be in the doghouse, with you at least."

"I'll say! In more ways than one." Ash came in close and whispered harshly, "I was covering for you, Thomas. While you went off to wherever—and then, you don't bother to *tell me* when you get back?! That'll make me look real great in my boss's eyes, if she ever finds out what I did."

"I don't know what you want me to say. Particularly in these close quarters." Thomas eyed the two officers who stood guard nearby.

Ash pulled away. "Look, I've gotta get moving so I can sit in on that interrogation. But first, you need to give me the bite-size version of what the hell was going on here—I assume this is your place?—or at least why Samantha Minn would run to *you* of all people after committing another murder."

"Who wants to know, Ash or Detective Westgard?"

"For now, the cop who's been sweating her ass off in all this gear. Just let me know what you've been up to today."

"Until a short while ago," Thomas said, "very little. I was relaxing here, with plans to dine at a nearby cafe later on, when Samantha called me frantically."

"From her loft, or was she already on the way over?"

"She was still at home then."

"What did she say was wrong? Could you see anything out of the ordinary when you spoke?"

Thomas shook his head. "She was just very upset and asked if we could meet. As her friend, naturally I agreed."

"Was her hair wet?"

"Yes, actually. Why?"

Ash said, "I figured she cleaned herself up before calling you."

"Oh," Thomas said quietly.

"So what happened after she got here?"

"First, she poured herself a drink and damn near gulped the entire thing down. Then she fell onto the couch and started bawling. I said to her, 'Sam, please, you have got to tell me what is the matter.' She looked up and said, 'I did it… again.' I couldn't believe, didn't want to believe…"

Thomas trailed off, his eyes becoming distant as he looked around the condominium which had been turned upside-down during the raid.

"But then what?" Ash said. "Did she expect you to help her escape? Offer an alibi? Or provide some sort of comfort? What the hell were you two doing in the bedroom anyway?"

"Who's asking *now?* You, or the lady in uniform?"

"Oh, come off it, Thomas! You don't owe me an explanation. We barely know each other, right?"

"It's not like that."

"And probably above my pay grade."

"What… ?"

"I'm sure you artsy types are just as incestuous as any other tight-knit group. Oh, how lovely it must have felt, to be caressed by hands still throbbing with the passion of a fresh kill!"

Thomas gave Ash a stern look. He raised his hands and said, "Untie me. Then I'll show you true passion."

She removed a utility knife from her pocket, snapping the blade open fiercely before ripping through the plastic tie.

Thomas checked his wrists to make sure he had not been cut, then stepped away from the kitchen. Ash followed him back into one of the bedrooms. He stopped in front of a watercolor painting that was near the window. In the piece, a young girl wearing a tattered ankle-length dress held a parasol above her head to shield herself from a rainstorm.

"It's just so enchanting," he said, then pointed to the bottom right corner. "Do you see that?"

Ash leaned in and read the artist's signature.

S. Minn

"Oh. Wow. One of her early works?"

"Precisely. Painted long before she lost her way,

or got too big of a head. This came purely from the heart, which is why I've always treasured it."

Ash said, "Did Samantha know the piece was here? Is that why she wanted to see you?"

"Not at all. She really was distraught. After I had finally gotten her to tell me everything that happened, it put her in such a frightful mood, and well… I have to admit, I was in a state of shock myself. For Sam to have killed Stanley, and then Dimitri, and afterward think of coming to *me!* I mean, you asked if I was an accessory or possibly the next victim… Perhaps those are logical concerns now, but in the moment I could only think of my poor friend. It was all crashing down around her, and she was absolutely devastated. So I brought her into the room, and together we admired this beautiful painting in silence. Until you and the cavalry arrived. Sadly, our reverie… that brief port in the storm for Samantha… has ended."

Thomas closed his eyes and turned away.

Ash was staring at the delicate angled lines of the rain streaks that Samantha Minn had painted many years ago.

In a voice that was barely audible, she said, "Someone will take you to the station for questioning. I'll… catch up with you later."

She bowed her head and left the room, unable to bring herself to look in Thomas's direction.

31. DERELICTION OF DUTY

"What if it's not the artist who's misunderstood? Unappreciated maybe, but otherwise the world understands them completely. Meaning that it's actually the artist who has misunderstood everyone else."

Samantha Minn leaned back and exhaled slowly through her lips.

"By holding everyone to a high standard. *Expecting* them to be honest and make all the right choices in life. But I guess we're naive. The world has never worked that way."

Ash said, "There's nothing wrong with being idealistic. Isn't art hopeful at its core?"

They were sitting across from each other inside a fortified interrogation room at police headquarters. She knew that other JPC officials were watching from behind the two-way glass on her left.

"I used to believe that," Samantha said. "But maybe it's not enough."

"Help me out here. How does this relate to why

you're in that chair?"

"You want me to explain *with words?!* Give me a block of wood and a chisel instead."

"I'm not sure we've got any chisels lying around the station, if you know what I mean. So let's talk it out instead."

"If you insist."

Ash sat back and appraised Samantha Minn. The woman had penetrating green eyes, a noble nose, straight and prominent upper teeth... and held her head high unflinchingly.

After a moment, Ash said, "It sounds to me like you were feeling frustrated as an artist. Maybe people weren't listening to your message? But from what I gather, that's a burden your profession has always had to deal with. Or... was it Stanley Bennett who faltered?"

"No, he didn't falter," Samantha replied. "He wanted to lead us further than we'd already gone."

"Did you resent him for taking charge like that?"

"Not at all. In fact, I sided with him whenever someone else wanted to slow down. I understood what he meant, what he stood for—even while my own work didn't keep pace. That's why... Surely he could see that I was trying! Otherwise, why would he be so obnoxious and bid on my sculpture like that?"

Ash recalled the murmurs on auction night when, early on in the bidding for Samantha's enormous walnut, Stanley Bennett had raised his hand once but then declined to make any further offers. She said, "Is it possible this was a gesture of affection or encouragement, or that even *he* was capable of a small lapse in judgment?"

Samantha looked off into the distance. She said, "You... might be right. But no, you're wrong! Because I was willing to let it go, especially after seeing how high the final bid went. Then I ran into Stanley later, and he toasted me by pointing at my piece and saying, 'Go big or go home, right?' The bastard! I felt as if he'd officially lost faith in me. Like my sculptures were some kind of cancerous tumor that grew in size to compensate for their lack of purpose."

"But how did you get him alone?" Ash pressed. "Surely he must have seen that you were offended?"

Samantha smiled. "I turned his attention away from me back to the object of his contempt. I led Stan over to the walnut and said, 'Let's have some fun.' I took out one of the birds, and as soon as he laughed, I knew he was game."

"Go on. What was your plan?"

"Mmm… No *plan*. Just a feeling. A thread of inspiration I was willing to follow."

"You left the main gallery, went into the hallway…"

"Yes, but it was crowded there, too. Everyone looking into the different studios and lining up outside the toilets. But a couple of the doors down at the end were shut tight. Of course, as M-24 members we both had electronic access, so that was no problem and he got us in. I said we should spruce up the bird and see how long it took for anyone to notice. He thought the idea was just brilliant, and drunkenly declared that this subversive act would surely liberate me from the blockage which had trapped me in my own creative birdcage."

Samantha nodded her head aggressively.

"And then?" Ash said.

"He selected a tube of acrylic paint from one of the carts, then handed it to me along with an old rag. He said, 'Samantha, do your damnedest.' So I did."

"You hit him, just like that?"

"Oh, no. I told him to look away while I worked so it would be a surprise. But even then, my conscious mind was just living in the moment—I really was prepared to dab a little paint on that bird and do nothing more. The problem was, like any dangerous idea you know you shouldn't even *indulge*, the waters kept pulling me along until it was too late to get out before reaching the falls."

"Were you talking to him the whole time while his back was turned?"

"Obviously. Not that I remember every little word that was spoken or—"

"That's a load of bull!" Ash snapped. "No way you didn't tell him exactly why you were about to do it."

Samantha Minn glanced up at the ceiling thoughtfully. She said, "I can see myself wrapping the rag around the bird. Stanley's bouncing around, he's so excited. His hands are over his eyes. He's saying how much fun this is going to be. I raise the bird. I say, 'Stan, it's ready!' He drops his arms and turns his head slowly, opens one eye... and bam! Just like that, he was down."

"And then you... ?"

"I smooched the bird and said, 'Thank you, my winged friend!' I tucked her and the paint tube inside my bag, then dropped the rag onto Stanley's face. When he didn't move, I nudged it down over his neck with my foot and gave it a tap. Still nothing, so I tapped a little harder. And again. Tap, tap, tap! A bit more and... Stomp and crush and not another word out of you! Going once... twice... and sold! Sold to the silence."

Samantha Minn's face broke its granite frame. Her mouth fell open and a heavy tear ran down her left cheek. She wiped it away absently.

"Sometimes you go cold, you know? The well of inspiration runs dry, but you still have to keep producing while you work through it. It's not *my* fault people kept buying the junk. I joined M-24 to improve! I wanted to feed off their energy and help the mission succeed."

Ash said, "But you have, Samantha. Has anyone said you don't belong?"

"It's not that. You have to know when to stop *pushing* someone and just offer silent support. But Stan couldn't stop, so even when he didn't actually say anything, his *work* still told the truth—that I was becoming a hack. I don't know, I suppose I could've endured it for the greater good. Maybe I should've just moved on to another studio. But the way he looked at my sculpture that night... I knew he'd lost all hope for me as a serious artist. He *pitied* me instead."

"But surely he held everyone else's feet to the fire, too? Or do you believe he was singling you out for ridicule? Because I saw how angry he got when Marta said she was leaving M-24. Maybe that bid was him rallying in support of you."

"We all know Marta's personality. It's annoying what she did, but not that surprising. With Stan, how he went about it is what I found so galling. Just be great, alright? Shine like the heavenly body everybody says you are, but don't stoop to our level! So yeah, he acted like one of us and played the silly human by bidding on my piece, and I punished him for it. Because he was better than that... and I was so terribly disappointed in him."

"Did he really deserve to die for that one indiscretion?"

"No," Samantha said quietly after a pause. "But artists, we're always playing with fire. He should've been more careful. But… oh. I see. He didn't think *I* had the fire anymore. That I was content to live off the gimmick. The worst part is, I might have to agree with that assessment."

Ash glanced down at her notes on the table. "When did you decide to deface the painting? What made you want to do that?"

"After he was dead, the rag slipped onto the floor and got some of his blood on it. I knew I'd have to get rid of it somehow. First I folded it up neatly so that the blood wouldn't show, but then there was a line for the bathrooms out in the hallway. Suddenly a group of people started dancing toward the music that was playing up front, and I just needed to get away from there so I joined them. We ended up going right past Stanley's painting, and while everyone else was watching them dance, I went up to it and hit the corner with the rag."

"And then?" Ash said.

"I went back to the bathrooms and said I really had to go. Somebody let me cut ahead of them and I flushed the rag down."

"Do you remember which unit it was?"

"Uh… Number three?"

"Okay. What did you do next?"

"I put the bird back on her perch. Her journey was complete!" Samantha's eyes sparkled.

"But not yours. You made a trip to the bar."

"I did. After the… the rush, I needed to calm down. And accept that I'd really done it. Then I could face whatever might happen."

"Did you expect to get caught immediately?"

"I don't know… But after they found him, I really did start to shut down. The rest of the night is a blur, and I'm being honest."

"I see. Where'd that tube of paint end up?"

"It's at home mixed in with my other supplies."

"You are a clever one. By the way, there's something I forgot to ask you when we first spoke on Saturday. Why the fascination with birds?"

A faint smile played across Samantha's lips. "My grandmother died after a long illness when I was eight years old. I used to visit her in the hospital, and together we would watch the birds nesting and playing outside her window. One day I decided to draw her a picture of them, and she adored it! So I kept going... and I've never stopped."

"That's a wonderful memory." Ash shuffled her papers, then said, "Let's move on and discuss Dimitri Kadnikov."

"Okay."

"I also met him at the gallery, and he seemed to love everybody."

"You're right," Samantha said, "he did."

"So... what happened at your loft that changed the mood from wine and cheese to you striking him down?"

"Wait. First I want to know how you found out about him so quickly."

Ash eased back in her chair and slung an arm over the top. "You know that, um, collector you were supposed to meet this afternoon? He was one of ours. We just had to re-route the squad after you ran off."

"I see," Samantha said grimly. "Today was going to be the day, no matter what."

"Pretty much. I do wish for Dimitri's sake that our decoy had been scheduled to arrive earlier. But life doesn't always go according to plan, right? Anyway, what'd you use to kill him?"

"Another bird, of course."

"Did you choke him out too?"

"No. I just kept hitting until he stopped

twitching."

"And where's that bird now? Did you hide it or toss it?"

"She got injured. I had to bury her."

"In the ground… or?"

"There was no time for a proper funeral. She rests in one of the trash cans for now."

"Inside your loft?"

Samantha nodded sadly.

"Now," Ash said, "go back and take me through it. What did Dimitri do, say, or *not say* to make you see red this time?"

"Well… He came by around two, because a write-up on my work which he'd arranged just came out in *Sculptors Quarterly*. It's a big deal and he wanted to congratulate me."

"Sounds good so far. Then what happened, did he make a pass at you?"

"God, no! His middle name ought to have been 'Propriety,' because he always knew when to stay in his own lane. Dimitri would never cross-pollinate with the talent."

"How very noble of him. So what was the problem?"

Samantha inhaled deeply. "Naturally, the topic of Stanley's passing came up. How could it not? Everyone's emotions were raw, and they were afraid because the killer was still out there." Her mouth quivered briefly. "Then Dimitri brought the conversation back around to me. My career, that is. He said now that Stanley was gone, maybe I could take center stage as M-24's new guiding light."

"That's not so bad," Ash said amiably. "Heck, you earned it by dethroning the king, right?"

"If I was an opportunistic snake! But my admiration for Stanley, as well as knowing my true place in the food chain, that didn't change just because I killed him. So for Dimitri to propose…"

"Are you saying *he* was being opportunistic in a sleazy way?"

"No, obviously that isn't his style. He offered me the kind of encouragement that Stanley couldn't give."

Ash blinked twice as her mouth fell open. She sputtered, "Isn't that exactly who you should have been listening to?"

"Absolutely not!" Samantha said with a cackle. "Because Stanley was right and Dimitri was wrong. Dimitri, by endlessly praising my mediocre work, was in essence passing out fake bills with my name on them. Did his unwavering support make me complacent? Did his words influence suggestible collectors into overpaying, so that the myth of Samantha Minn corrupted us all?"

"Look, if you felt that Stan had insulted you, I can understand why you might lose your cool. But to murder one of your biggest champions?"

Samantha pointed a finger at Ash and said, "Do you know what separates artists from critics? *We* have to create. But a critic chooses that role. No one asked *them* to weigh in! Still, the task itself is noble. It's a great responsibility to act as both gatekeeper and intermediary. Which is why I say that Dimitri Kadnikov was guilty of dereliction of duty. He failed in his obligation to art itself."

"That's some tough talk, but did you ever actually call him out on it before? Because I assume you never turned down any of those fat checks his influence brought in."

"You just don't get it, you peasant! It's always interlopers like you who spoil the arts."

"Me?" Ash said incredulously. "I didn't buy a damn thing on Saturday. Had never even heard of you before coming face to face with that ridiculous walnut."

Samantha smirked. "That's how it starts, though. Newbies wander into our sanctuary, get caught up in the excitement, and then they want to brush up against us. Feel the warm glow, get a taste of our glory."

Ash leaned forward onto her elbows. Quietly, she said, "I'm not trying to steal your thunder, Samantha. Believe it or not, I've been in the spotlight a few times myself. On a smaller scale than you all, of course. But I get that it's hard to stay true to yourself when everyone's telling you *yes*, no matter what you do or say."

Samantha eyed Ash critically for a moment, then said, "Your face, it's very beautiful. I can see how people might try to possess you."

"Come on now. The last thing I need is another yes." Ash gave a small smile.

"I could sculpt your bust in clay. I already see it in my mind. What a shame I didn't pay you more attention that night. Who knows, maybe I'd have found a new path forward, and a way to break free. Then none of that unpleasantness would have happened, and Stanley might still be alive."

"Dimitri, too."

"Yes, well. A lot of things would have turned out differently."

32. BLANK CANVAS

"Nice work."

A tired-looking Chief Paraquez gave Ash a pat on the shoulder.

"All in a day's… something," she replied.

The women moved slowly down the corridor. A digital display above their heads indicated it was nearly ten o'clock.

Paraquez said, "That was one slick operation, if I do say so myself. JPC is really up to the task."

"It all starts with the right leadership," Ash said politely. "Especially those who stay close to the action."

"I appreciate that, and your dedicated work this week. It felt great to be out there with the team, but now I've got to switch back into the e-suite mindset. Prepare a public statement, send a summary of events upstairs, and of course get the case details organized for Samantha's trial."

"Where do you think she'll end up?"

"That's a good question," Paraquez mused. "I'm

not sure that having multiple murders on her rap sheet would sit well with the residents of a crafts colony. But her creative talents shouldn't be allowed to go to waste in a dreg-zone, either."

"Although," Ash said, "she might actually feel at home down there. No bots to compete against."

"It's possible, but not my call. We'll feed in all the data and let the system calculate her options. Let's hope that whatever flesh-and-bone attorney represents her has the wherewithal to work every nuance in her favor."

"Are you going soft on me, Chief? After the grind we just pulled?"

Paraquez shrugged her shoulders. "I could use a touch of grace in the aftermath of victory. Because, you know, being a part of society's clean-up crew… sometimes I worry about the smell sticking to us. Anyway, you've earned a night off. Time to clock out."

"Cheers, boss. G'night."

"See you on the other side, Detective Westgard."

Ash gave the chief a quick salute, then headed in the direction of the nearest coffee dispenser. She needed a few minutes to decompress by herself before getting cleaned up and heading home.

But as she went past a small waiting area, Ash came face to face with Jo Green and Thomas Templeton. The gears in her head immediately started turning…

"What are *you guys* up to?"

Jo, who was still wearing tactical gear except for her jacket, said, "Figured you'd want to have a word with this one before we cut him loose."

"Do I?" Ash gave the seated Thomas a doubtful look. "What's he had to say for himself so far?"

"Nothing I can relate to. I don't think he's ever seen the inside of a precinct before."

Thomas raised a finger. "May I?"

"By all means," Ash said.

"I have provided a statement, and answered every question as truthfully as possible. They told me I was free to go. Your partner here indicated otherwise."

"And where were you off to? Back to the condo, or your island paradise?"

"I could hardly return *there*. Someone smashed in my door and ransacked the place, didn't you hear?"

Ash shot Jo a glance, taking an extra moment to fix on her eyes. She said, "Well, Officer Green. It seems as if Mr. Templeton has nowhere to lay his head tonight. What *ever* shall we do?"

"I didn't say—" Thomas began, but Jo cut him off.

"Ahhh, that's right. And a man in *those* fancy pants might be an easy target for the predators out in the streets."

"Do you suppose he needs a police escort?" Ash said.

"Definitely. Safety first!"

"Now Jo, you wouldn't happen to, uh, be free to work that shift on such short notice, would you? Strictly off the books, of course."

"Mmm… I could *maybe* squeeze it into my schedule." Jo smirked and added, "Just lemme go put on my undercover uniform."

As Jo walked away with a bounce in her step, Thomas looked up at Ash and said, "What's going on here?"

She moved closer to him and nudged a knee against his. "You're about to enter my *other* world. As long as it's not already past your bedtime."

"With your friend as chaperon or accomplice?"

"Heh, yeah. Truth is, I don't really know her all that well. *Yet.*"

Thomas gave a small grumble, then said, "Are you hinting that I now have competition?"

"Maaaaybe?" Ash slit her eyes. "Or, could be that everyone gets a trophy tonight."

"My god…"

Ash held out her hand. Thomas took it and rose from his seat.

"Come on," she said, looking up at his face. "I don't believe for a second that a world-weary man like you could still be *that* innocent."

"You really are set on damning my soul, aren't you? To keep me trapped in this fallen world forever."

"Or, I'm just trying to get you out of your head and into the moment." She leaned in close, but felt his body stiffen with resistance as she breathed, "I know how to make you forget your own name…"

He pulled away and declared, "Listen here. I most certainly intend to go along with you two Erica she-beasts, right on down to the wickedest depths of whatever pit you call a nest. But while you gleefully attempt to corrupt this little schoolboy, just remember that *I* know things, too."

"*Oh?* Do tell… and show!" Ash pretended to swoon and fanned at her face.

"No, Ashley, you misunderstand. I know how things *work*. And not the mere manipulation of bodily functions, either. I refer to the mechanics of the wider world—even if I personally have bowed out from reaching the potentialities afforded by my birthright."

Ash was now truly taken aback. "What… are you saying exactly?"

"It could be that I'm matching you threat for threat in an arms race of bold claims."

"Hmm. Kinda sounds like you're negotiating a deal. But is it with me, the devil, or your own conscience?"

"Truth be told," Thomas said, "alliances and common interests are often what make the world go round. *And* keep everyone in check."

"So… I'm your new *ally?* That doesn't have quite the same ring as 'girlfriend,' now does it?"

Thomas's face softened as he smiled. "But such a relationship might prove to have a longer shelf life. Anyone can be shocked or dazzled by some novelty—and in turn, captivate others with the tricks they've just learned. But imagine not living so passively, where existence then becomes much more than simply being the recipient of favors and traumas. *That* is what I'm proposing."

Ash felt a momentary flash of dizziness. She blinked several times and stammered, "I don't even…"

"Mysteries!" Thomas pronounced. "We are all starved for a bit of mystery in this constricting age. The shrouded truths we sense are there, and which hold so much sway over our daily lives, but still we rarely get to see or touch. Perhaps you and I will journey behind the curtain together and explore some of these great secrets…"

Just then, they caught sight of Jo Green sauntering down the hall. She looked fetching in a red-and-navy plaid snap shirt with shiny silver accents and cut-off denim shorts. The cop in sweaty combat gear had transformed into a pigtailed cowgirl.

"Say," she drawled, "any of y'all got an extra ticket to the rodeo?"

Ash leaned against Thomas and he put an arm around her shoulder. They fell into step and went to meet Jo.

Their second date had officially begun, with a spunky third wheel along for the ride. The night that lay ahead was a perfectly blank canvas…

33. EPILOGUE

At dusk several days after the investigation ended, Ash rode her ATV to Stanley Bennett's makeshift memorial in the Jacksonville Arts District. Flowers, mementos, and handwritten notes surrounded the large black-and-white photograph of the deceased artist.

No one else was around.

She approached the shrine, kneeling briefly to place her own tribute: one of the silver high heels she had worn on that fateful Saturday night at the gallery.

"And I'm keeping the other one," she said. "To remember what could've been."

She turned to shield her face from a passing gust of wind, unsure of whether to stay now that she had made the gesture.

"I'm sorry about everything," she heard herself say suddenly. "Sorry for the people who already miss you. Sorry that a guy who loved what he did had to leave so young. And I'm sorry that the only reason I got to know you was because you died."

Ash zipped her jacket closed, then pulled on a pair of cotton gloves as the air cooled.

"But that's my deal. My process. The facts only get you so far. Now, the person… If I can figure out who the person really was, maybe I'll understand why they became a *victim*. It's not always textbook, or pretty, but there's still a locker with my name on it at JPC, so I guess I'm doing something right.

"You know, you challenged me. I had to get *sharper* to find out who the hell it was that cut you down. Sounds like that's the kind of thing you would have wanted, though. For me and everybody else."

Ash heard a noise and shot a glance to her left. A young couple was approaching on the sidewalk, each holding a tall glass candle in their hand.

Turning back to Stanley's picture, she said quietly, "Time to say goodbye. But maybe I'll take you out on the job with me sometime. Deal? See you around, Mr. Bennett."

She stepped away as the others arrived, then gunned her ATV down the road and out of sight.

THE END.

*If you enjoyed this story
and would like to see
Ash's adventures continue,
please visit the website
where you purchased the
book and post a review.*

ABOUT THE AUTHOR

Originally from Northern Virginia, Philip Wyeth has lived in the Los Angeles area for many years. He's an entrepreneur, musician, film aficionado, hockey fan, and enjoys playing tennis and golf.

Inspired by such unique writers as Heinrich von Kleist, Ambrose Bierce, Joseph Conrad, and Len Deighton, Wyeth's imaginative and insightful novels will resonate with fans of Philip K. Dick, Michel Houellebecq, Harry Harrison, George Orwell, Robert Sheckley, and Bruce Sterling.

Also a lifelong fan of heavy metal music and its many sub-genres, Wyeth strives to infuse his writing with comparable levels of intensity, independence, and larger-than-life visions.

His website is www.philipwyeth.com, and you can follow him across the social media landscape under the following handles:

@PhilipWyeth: Twitter, BitChute, Gab, and Minds.

@PhilipWyethWriter: Instagram and Facebook.